I0457767

Wicked Obsession

Cora Zane

Grrl X Publishing

Wicked Obsession
Copyright © Cora Zane 2011
All rights reserved.

ISBN-13: 978-0692254639
ISBN-10: 0692254633

Cover Layout by CDT Designs
Stock: the red mask, © Can Stock Photo Inc. / carlodapino
Edited by Carolyn Pinard Consults
Formatted by Polgarus Studio

This is a work of fiction. Names, characters, places, and incidents are products of the author's imagination or are used fictitiously and are not to be construed as real. Any resemblance to actual events, locales, organizations, or persons, living or dead, is entirely coincidental.

No part of this book may be used or reproduced electronically or in print without written permission, except in the case of brief quotations embodied in reviews.

Special thanks are in order. Cheers to author Elise Hepner for the late night chats that have kept me motivated and inspired, and to beta reader Linnea Hall McCain, Queen of Awesomeness, for her eagle eye and rapid reading skills. Ladies, you rock!

Chapter One

At ten minutes before midnight on January 27th, the hearing to determine Eleni Audridov's fate began. Sick with nervousness and a jangling sense of heart-weary anticipation, she stood before the vampire council and forced herself not to hang her head in shame.

Dressed conservatively in a sleek black dress, her long hair flowing over her shoulder like a cascade of moonlight, she struggled to appear aloof, indifferent, as shrewd eyes—doubtful eyes—studied her from across the ancient boardroom table set up in front of a grand fireplace. Whatever the outcome, if she managed nothing else tonight, she had to at least appear put-together and calm; both for her sake, and for her sister, Anya's.

On Wednesday, she'd received the summons. She'd been called to the private home of a society vampire located in Nob Hill, and she would only be allowed one representative. Her brother-in-law, Dominic Lisandro, had agreed he must go with her. If the council would listen, he planned to speak on her behalf. It was Eleni's hope that his family name and the honorable history of his bloodline would be enough to afford her a lighter sentence than the one she expected to receive.

Together, they waited in the crackling silence of the library for the Regent Elect, who sat looking exceptionally grim and unimpressed, to begin the hearing. Seven other vampires had gathered with him to determine her future.

As an Acolyte, a human born into vampire society and groomed from a young age to be a companion and potential mate for a vampire, it was the only life she knew. Eleni didn't know what she would do if they cut her off from society or forbade her from having any contact with vampires.

Her sister was newly turned, blood bound to Dominic. For the past year, Eleni had lived in their household while they took care of her and helped her recover from Biter's Addiction. Such a verdict would cut her off from the only family she had. The idea was more terrifying than death.

She had nearly lost everything to Zander Rubio, her former Biter. He had attempted to take her fortune, her inheritance, her sanity, and her life. She tried not to think about him, about all the pain he had caused, but that was a little like trying not to breathe. When he'd abandoned her, it had nearly driven her to madness. The Biter's Addiction had all but consumed her by that point. She had not only craved his bite, but in the darkest moments of her addiction, she had craved the pain he inflicted on her as well.

Through it all she had battled a growing sense of desperation and paranoia. It embarrassed her to think of it now, how desperate she'd been to feel the thrilling physical connection of his fangs. Knowing he had infected her on purpose still made her wince with shame and heartache. She'd been helpless then, so very weak.

She was much better now, but her life was far from perfect. She'd come out of those dark days aware that it would take a long time to heal her emotional scars—if they ever healed at all. Rubio's abuse and greed had left her desolate, her ability to trust broken. Even though she wasn't in love with him anymore, she had been with him for so long, she felt lost without him. Like there was a great gaping hole in her heart. Even now, the frightening emptiness of being rejected in the most brutal way lingered. Eleni accepted the possibility that she might never get over what he had done to her.

To her left, and across the room, her sister Anya watched in pensive silence. Ethereal and blond, she sat with a handful of witnesses that included a medical specialist serving the San Francisco vampire community, an historical archivist, and Vladimir Lechenko—the owner of the house that served as her courtroom.

Her sister looked pale and angelic in her immortality. Her cool blue eyes were a comfort to Eleni, even now. Anya looked much like their mother, what little Eleni remembered of her. Ever since she was a little girl, her big sister had represented home and safety. Now that was at risk. Emotions running high, a lump formed in her throat.

She swallowed thickly and took a deep breath to regain her composure, trying to soothe herself with the knowledge that her sister would live forever. No matter what happened, the council couldn't take that away from her.

On the other hand, one black mark on the Audridov line, and the taint of shame would leave an indelible mark on their familial line. And Biter's Addiction was a shame that had far reaching roots, part of the reason Dominic was so willing to become involved in her welfare, Eleni was sure. Anything representing a danger to Anya's bloodline could very well represent a danger to his own.

Regardless of his reason for attempting to place her under the protection of his name, she was grateful. He and Anya had done so much for her already. If not for both of them, she imagined she would have been turned out in disgrace by now, and would likely be living on the streets.

The council had patiently waited until she had recovered from Biter's Addiction before appointing this meeting. Whatever sentence they planned against her, it would be life-altering. Dominic told her Grigori Vidam was fair, but he was also a stickler for vampire law. Yes, the Audridov family bloodline had run red through vampire society for countless generations, but her transgressions against the Acolyte code could make that a moot point. For that reason, Dominic had refused to speculate where she could end up after this evening. The council's decision could go either way.

Grigori Vidam cleared his throat, and opened a large leather book in front of him. A strip of silk marked a specific page. Eleni's heart raced when she realized the heavy tome was the Book of Acolytes. The name of every Acolyte, and their date of birth, was recorded in the archives. A record was kept of their life and death, including information on their Biter, if they were sponsored by a bloodline, and if any child was born to them befitting the heritable title of Acolyte. Her stomach churned at the thought of her failures as an Acolyte being listed forever on those pages. That would be her legacy— the shame and disgrace she brought on her family name. It stripped her pride bare and tore at her heart.

The Elder vampire looked across the table at her and called the hearing to order. Vidam was a burly man, middle-aged, with thin, prickly brown hair shaved to the scalp, and a slightly ruddy complexion. His unattractiveness was very unusual for a vampire, especially one of such high rank. Despite his looks, he held himself like the noble he was, and Eleni Audridov did not miss the way he looked down his broad nose at her. His piercing blue eyes weighed her worth.

He then turned his gaze on Dominic. His deep, rumbling voice was made all the more authoritative by his heavy Russian accent. "What interest do you have in this Acolyte, Lisandro?"

"Eleni is the sister of my bloodmate," Dominic stated for the record.

The burly Russian eyed her with curt appraisal. "Your breeding is evident," he remarked in a dry tone. "You have the look of your sister. Audridov is an old line, am I correct?"

"It can be traced back several centuries," she admitted quietly.

Vidam asked Dominic, "She is not one of your protégés?"

"No. But she has been in my care since being recovered from Zander Rubio's harem."

The Regent Elder bent his head and began to write notes in the margin of the book. "Ms. Audridov, how long did you live as Rubio's protégé?

"I was his *premiere* protégé," she corrected him, "for more than two years. I was also his fiancée for six months. It was during that time I became...*ill.*"

Grigori's brows lifted. "I'm aware of your grievance with Rubio. I have statements on the record which state he promised to make you his bloodmate, and took a sizeable dowry from you. I am also aware of his attack on your sister, prompted by a fit of rage when he was forced to return that dowry. Tonight, however, we must figure out what to do with you. As far as I'm concerned, no one is innocent in this circus of reprehensible behavior shared by you and your former Biter."

The shame was nearly unbearable. Eleni swallowed hard, but said nothing as she swiped at the tears that stung her eyes.

Grigori scribbled more notes while saying to her, "Very few Acolytes who have been stricken with Biter's Addiction have managed to recover completely. It appears you have come a long way in a year, but you will always need careful handling to prevent a relapse. And there is always the chance of passing it to your children." He studied her face. "What do you say about that?"

"I wish I could change the past," she said tremulously. "I wish I hadn't been such a fool. Rubio took advantage of my feelings for him." She shook her head. "I know he is not entirely to blame, but I...wanted to make him happy. I can't see how it could have turned out different with us, because he was never honest with me. He deliberately...compromised me...to take advantage of me for financial gain. I am far wiser now than I was a year ago. But I must confess, at the time, I would have done anything to please him. But that is hardly my fault alone. Rubio knew I was vulnerable, and he took advantage of me."

"It was your responsibility to know your limits, and also to say no to your Biter, to protect yourself and your bloodline. You have been grossly irresponsible. Zander Rubio is only partly to blame. It's an Acolyte's duty to make smart and beneficial decisions. Everything he or she does, affects not only him or herself, but also impacts your future bloodline. You know this. These facts have been ingrained in you since childhood. Your deplorable decision making, your risky behavior, has not only brought shame to your family name, but has likely ruined any chance you might have had of ever entering a blood bond."

"And I will accept that." Eleni bowed her head.

"How noble of you," Vidam sneered, the action giving her a brief glimpse of his fangs. "Do you believe Zander Rubio feels the same as you? That he is willing to wallow about in self-degradation while his name and that of his ancestors is sullied and diminished?" He gestured up to the balcony box, on the second floor of the library.

She glanced up to the place where he indicated and felt a quick, wincing shock when she saw her former Biter watching her from a little glassed-in office. Of course, the council wouldn't permit him in the room during her hearing. But, since he had faced charges for his abuses against her, it was his right to sit through her trial to learn of the outcome.

"His sentence was quite severe, Ms. Audridov. Like me, he couldn't care less about any personal sense of regret you may have."

Eleni didn't tell him she hadn't gone to Rubio's trial. She'd been too sick at the time and under constant supervision. Still, his tone put her teeth on edge. "Zander made his bed—"

"As have you, with your lack of judgment," Vidam snapped. "Was it not in your power as an Acolyte to refuse his fangs? To tell him you would not accept the bite of any other vampire? I can only imagine the gross number of times he and others must have bitten you daily to produce such an illness. Your disgrace is only the beginning of this problem, do you see? If I were to allow you to retain your status, where would I even place you? What Biter would have you in his house, much less his harem? You've been ill used. You're damaged goods, Ms. Audridov. This is the problem, and I'm left to wonder if it would even be worth the effort."

"Julian de Sevigne is prepared to take her into his household," Dominic interjected.

Vidam's gaze snapped to his face. He scoffed. "Sevigne? You've been in contact with him? One would think him dead considering his lack of interaction with the outside world. Where is he living now?"

"Where he has always lived, I would imagine—in the Sévigné chateau. The family lands in the Périgord Pourpre are still his." Dominic gestured his indifference with a wave of his hand. "More importantly, he's aware of Eleni's delicate condition. He's agreed to take her in regardless of her status. He's a traditionalist, and will pay careful attention to her requirements. I will stake my blood name on that as truth. As Eleni's current guardian, I have accepted his offer, bearing the council's decision, of course."

The Regent Elder's eyes glittered in cold calculation as he silently contemplated what Dominic said. Finally, he took a deep breath, his mouth drawn down at the corners, and picked up his pen. He wrote in the Book of Acolytes for several minutes. Turned a delicate, razor-fine page, and wrote some more.

Eleni glanced over at Anya, who watched her with fear in her blue eyes. Finally, Vidam put down his pen and sighed deeply. He closed the huge leather book.

"Very well. If it satisfies everyone involved, Ms. Audridov shall be placed into the care of Master Vampire Julian de Sévigné of France. But consider this a probationary arrangement to be revisited in four months." His hard expression never wavered. "Make no mistake, Ms. Audridov, if you have not truly mastered your illness, if you cannot prove to me in four months' time that you can readapt to the lifestyle of an Acolyte, both as a lover and a donor, I will not hesitate to place you in permanent disgrace and sever you from your bloodline. Doing so will place a black mark against the Audridov name. I hope you keep that in mind. Biter's Addiction runs in families. The family lines are like a garden—weeds must sometimes be plucked to ensure the health of the rest of the crop. You will be watched closely, am I understood?"

She swallowed hard. "Clearly."

"Then so it is written," the Regent Elder announced to the room. "This hearing is adjourned."

Numb to the core, Eleni could barely breathe. It hadn't yet settled in—the full implication of the verdict. Dominic threaded his arm through hers and quickly led her away toward the door, stopping only to wait for Anya, who was heading toward them, sobbing into a handkerchief, her eyes -red-rimmed and brimming with tears.

It could have been much worse, but it still wasn't over. Eleni's heart sank like a stone as her sister embraced her and rambled in her ear that it would all be okay. Dominic allowed his wife a moment, then took her by the shoulders and directed her toward the door. "We really should get out of here."

Eleni followed them across the room and was right behind Dominic when Grigori Vidam called out to her.

"Eleni Audridov."

She halted at the door and turned. Dread pooled like blood in the core of her stomach. The room had grown suddenly silent. Vidam's piercing gaze sent a shiver down her spine.

"Know that had it not been for Dominic, you would be stripped of your status right now, and removed from society. This is an opportunity very few Acolytes would have been granted in the same situation." His serious expression turned grave. "Do not think to take advantage of my generosity."

She swallowed hard, and bowed her head in respect. "I wouldn't dream of it."

"I suppose we will know when we see each other again in May," he challenged.

Eleni frowned as heat swept across her face. Embarrassed, she wondered if Rubio had seen Vidam's slight. She glanced up at the balcony box overlooking the library floor. Zander Rubio wasn't paying attention to her at all. He was arguing violently with two members of his household, and a reddish-haired man whose face she couldn't see.

Chapter Two

France

Twilight fell over the patchwork landscape of Ville Cleménce. It was late Sunday, and a light snow fell in silent swirls from the darkening sky. Eleni held her breath as the charter plane touched down on the private runway. The flight from Paris seemed almost like a dream, numb and colorless, as if she were suspended in a world of gray. The bouncy landing drew her back to the real world, and as the plane finally slowed and exited the runway, Eleni sat straighter. On the edge of the frosty tarmac, a limo waited. The plane rolled to a stop, and she anxiously stared out her window until the co-pilot drew her attention. He had let down the side-steps so she could disembark, and was waving her forward.

She paused for a moment to pull on her red wool coat, then took down the travel bag she'd carried onboard with her. She walked up the aisle and ducked her blonde head to peer out of the charter plane. The world had been wiped clean with a thin layer of snow. She hoped it was an omen for the future. Stepping off of the plane, her breath frosted white on the cold air. The co-pilot waited for her at ground level, and held a hand out to help her step carefully down to the pavement.

A limousine with dark tinted windows was parked at the side of the runway. Seeing it, she felt a brief stab of panic. The car wasn't a surprise, but the possibility that Julian had come for her himself startled her. She hadn't considered he might do that.

As she started across the tarmac, the door of the car opened and an elderly man of average height and build stepped out. There was nothing remarkable to remember him by, other than the gaunt, if somewhat rosy, face. He wore a black beret pulled low over his eyes, black driving gloves, and a buttoned up pea coat in a dreary shade of brown. Unassuming and anonymous, he was the kind of man you could lose easily in a crowd.

He didn't come forward to greet her. Instead, he shouted something in French to the co-pilot and went around to the back of the car, opening the trunk for her luggage, which the men were now carrying from the plane.

Eleni followed the driver. "Julian?"

"*Non, Mademoiselle.* Henri." He tapped his chest with a gloved finger. "I drive you to Master Julian's chateau."

Eleni stepped out of the way as the pilot and the co-pilot, two healthy looking middle-aged men, brought her bags around to the back of the car. They set some of them in the trunk, the others they set down near Henri's feet.

The pilot left first, his gaze roving over her briefly before he stalked off toward the plane. The co-pilot lingered. He exchanged a few brief words in French with Henri, words that Eleni couldn't interpret, then the tan, gray haired man laughed and gave Henri a hearty pat on the back before he started toward the plane. Henri placed the last two cases in the back of the car. Eleni watched him, shivering in the cold, not sure whether she should go ahead and get in the car or wait for him.

"Come, *Mademoiselle.*"

He walked her around the car and opened the door for her, and she took a step forward. When she glimpsed an open fur coat and crossed legs in sheer stockings, she hesitated. Her gaze jumped to see the face, but it was concealed beneath a large hat with a black veil. Without a doubt, the woman was a vampiress.

"Enter or shut the door," the woman said in a thick French accent. Eleni slid into the seat. The interior of the car smelled of rich leathers and the fading crispness of the cold air. Henri closed the door for her, sealing her in, and Eleni swept her hair from her eyes. It took her vision a moment to adjust to the darkness of the car.

The woman drew back the veil and removed her hat, revealing a wealth of sleek, auburn hair and delicate, pale features. Her lips were painted a bright matte red.

"Welcome, Eleni." The tips of her fangs gleamed like little pearls when she spoke, and Eleni jumped when the woman leaned forward and greeted her with a kiss on both cheeks. The vampiress pulled back, her eyes sparkling like emeralds. "I am Marguerite de Sévigné. Julian sent me to pick you up this evening. I hope you don't mind. He rarely leaves the chateau these days."

"You live with Julian?" Eleni asked. The woman dazzled her with a smile.

"I have my own chateau, and my own harem to care for. Julian is a cousin. We're separated by centuries, and several generations, of course." The car was moving, and for a moment, she glanced out at the landscape scrolling by. "Men, they are demanding souls, you know? I don't think it ever changes for them, regardless of age." She laughed softly. "Julian is no different. When he needs something his servants cannot provide, he calls on me to do what I can."

"You're lovers? You and Julian?" Eleni asked, unable to hide her shock.

Marguerite laughed, then reached over and patted Eleni on the thigh. "Ah, Eleni…as much as I adore my dear Julian, I could not put up with him to that extent. No, he's not my lover. I'm afraid that role will be left entirely up to you."

That was a relief. She nodded, but her face was hot and red from her faux pas. She wasn't really sure what else to say or think. There seemed to be a double entendre in almost everything the vampiress said. She fiercely hoped that Marguerite and Julian were not lovers. She'd been told that he had no harem, but he had to have a blood source. Eleni hadn't anticipated this new worry. The Sévignés were from old aristocratic stock, and vampires had their own rules regarding relationships. It was not unheard of for cousins to enter an arranged marriage in an effort to keep the bloodline pure.

The vampiress reached out and took her hand, and Eleni jumped, even though the gesture was gentle enough. Marguerite's skin was cool and smooth as silk. Her nails were long and red, and filed to perfect ovals, so very different from Eleni's hands. Perhaps the woman found humor in Eleni's French manicure. She had no idea what the woman was thinking when she turned her hand palm up, exposing her wrist. The vampiress traced a long red nail over the fine blue veins beneath Eleni's pale skin, making her shiver.

A curious smile curved Marguerite's lips as she laid Eleni's hand back in her lap. "You are the very essence of loveliness." Those magnetic green eyes pierced Eleni's own. It seemed they held a thousand secrets. "Yes, I do believe you will be to Julian's liking."

They drove east into the hills along a narrow, winding road, and when Eleni looked off to her right, down in the valley below, she could see the actual village for which the area was named. It looked like something out of a photograph, a dense cluster of stone buildings with slate gray roofs dusted with snow. She studied the peaks and angles of the buildings until a stand of trees blocked her view. By then they had rounded a deep curve, and the village disappeared from view as the car turned north.

Five minutes later, Marguerite pointed up the hill to her left. "Le Chateau du Sévigné." Eleni barely glimpsed a segment of gray stone before the trees thickened and obscured it from view. A short distance later, the land leveled out and the landscape opened into a sleeping vineyard arranged in stark rows, the wooden trellising poking through the snow.

"All of this," Marguerite gestured toward the scene scrolling past the window, "every hectare, is Julian's. You have heard of Sévigné wines?"

"I have," she said, and it was not entirely a lie. Dominic told her Julian was a vigneron, although admittedly, she hadn't given it much thought. Her former Biter had lived off investments and gifts from the Acolytes in his sizeable harem. She had been one of those women providing financial gifts, and even now, the memory of it upset her. Before his fall, Zander Rubio had lived a life of privilege off the backs of others. On the other hand, the way Marguerite spoke of the land and its history, the vineyard was clearly a matter of pride to the family. Still, the mere thought of Rubio agitated her. Eleni frowned at the sudden rise of anxiety. Her hands shook. She tucked them into the folds of her coat to keep Marguerite from noticing, but it was too late.

"You are nervous?" Marguerite asked.

"A little. It's been years since I last visited France."

Marguerite laughed. "Nothing changes that much." She turned her head, her eyes shifting color yet again as the car passed under the shadows of trees, making the interior even darker. "No matter where you go, it is the same. You will see."

It took another ten minutes to reach the chateau. They wound their way up the hill, and when the drive leveled out, Henri turned off onto a narrow road marked *privé*. They passed the shelter of snow-laden evergreens, and at the end of the paved drive, the mansion sat regally overlooking the estate. It looked like something straight out of a fairy tale, three stories of old stone with twin turrets capped with gray, pointed roofs. It was lit both inside and out so that it glowed in the early nightfall.

Henri drove directly into the attached garage and killed the engine. Eleni's insides churned with anxiety.

"Don't worry about the bags. Henri will take care of everything," Marguerite said, excitement in her voice. She threw open the car door and smiled, showing a flash of fangs. "Come. I'm excited for you to meet Julian."

Eleni didn't know what to expect. Nerves frazzled, she stumbled a little when she climbed out of the backseat. Marguerite caught her arm to steady her, and heat blazed across Eleni's face.

"I'm sorry, I—"

"You are shivering." Marguerite frowned. "We must get you into the house."

She couldn't afford to show any signs of imbalance while here. Not with Grigori's probation hanging over her head. She mustn't give them any reason to doubt her ability to do her duty.

Marguerite waited at the door for her, and they went together through a heavy black door while Henri walked around to the trunk of the car for her baggage.

"It's dark," Eleni said. She kept her hand on the wall to keep from stumbling.

"This is the master's passage. It's shielded from sunlight. No windows. It leads from the garage to the main foyer. Or, if you take a right a little further down the corridor, it will take you to the kitchens. There is also a staircase a little farther down the passage and on the left. It leads up to the west wing of the house, where your bedroom will be."

"How many people live here?"

"There is Julian and three members of his serving staff. You met Henri. He lives in the *gîte rural* not far from the chateau. There is also Giselle and Claudette. Claudette— she's the main housekeeper and cook. If you need something, you will take it up with her before going to Julian. He's often busy with the running of the vineyard. Although he has employed workers from the village to take care of the day labor, there is the business side of things he must attend to. But do not worry, Julian will sort it all out with you. It will all seem like second nature soon enough."

Marguerite opened a door at the end of the passage and placed a hand on Eleni's back, urging her to go through. Eleni stepped across the threshold and froze at the sight of an elaborate twin staircase. It seemed to embrace the enormous room. Behind the railing of the central balcony on the floor above, a stained glass window in jewel tones of blues, purples, reds, and greens depicted a sorrowful man in robes holding a book, a millstone around his neck. Around the figure were grapevines laden with fruit, and four ravens with ribbon banners unfurling from their mouths. A chill came over her when she looked into the disapproving eyes of the saint.

"St. Vincent of Saragossa," Marguerite said, gesturing to the window. "He's the patron saint of *vignerons*. In a way, he is the symbol of the Sévigné vineyards. The raven is a part of our family crest."

Marguerite tossed her handbag onto a heavy-limbed chair and started across the foyer in long, sure strides, her heels clicking over the chocolate marble.

"Julian!" she called out, her voice echoing through the house as she slipped into the shadowed hallway beneath the interior balcony.

Overwhelmed by the house and a sudden unsettling feeling, almost a kind of dark presentiment, Eleni watched her go. Heart racing, she watched the vampiress knock briefly before poking her head around a door. Muffled voices in French, then Marguerite leaned away from the door and looked straight at her, her eyes reflecting like two green rings in the shadows.

"Eleni, this way." Marguerite's voice echoed down the hall. Reluctantly, Eleni passed beneath the balcony and St. Vincent's window to join the vampiress who waited for her outside a set of arched double doors.

"You can go in. He's ready to see you."

Eleni swallowed thickly. She'd never been so nervous in her life. Since her early childhood, she had been told tales of the mal vampires, the dangerous ones, the ill-bred and infirm ones. Sometimes they were the vampires created too old to be aesthetically pleasing, or in Julian's case, a vampire whom had been damaged in a way that had made it impossible for him to heal perfectly.

Whatever the reason for a mal vampire's imperfection, they were considered unpresentable in appearance for both human and vampire society. Dominic had warned her that long ago Julian had been in a fire, that he'd been burnt beyond recognition. It had taken him years to recover, but the healing had not been perfect. Even Dominic had not known the extent of his injuries, but Eleni had a good idea of how bad it must be if he hid himself away in this isolated chateau. Then again, when she entered the room, the only person sitting there was a man watching her from behind a large, teak desk, and he looked nothing like a mal vampire.

Long hair the color of midnight draped over his shoulders, and his piercing gray eyes followed her as she came in to stand before him. He looked at her down a proud nose that gave him an air of regal distinction. She was immediately intimidated.

All this time she'd expected a monster, and this man was hardly that. She resisted the urge to glance around the room for someone else in case she had made a mistake.

He was gorgeous, dressed in an expensive black sweater. He eyed her with barely shielded disdain when

Marguerite led her forward, her hands on her shoulders as if to present a teacher with a new star pupil.

"Julian, this is your new Acolyte, Eleni. We had a pleasant ride, I think."

Eleni nodded. "It's a pleasure to meet you." When he said nothing in response, Eleni threw a questioning glance at Marguerite. She tried again. "I'm grateful you have taken me into your household."

"Gratitude implies that you are not to be held to the rules of my house. Let us get one thing straight right now—this arrangement is not a favor to you, or to your brother-in-law. Dominic gave you to me as a blood gift. To be used. And you will be used—just as you have used the security of my house to escape the superficial shame of the vampire council."

Julian's remark struck her like an open palm. A sharp silence fell across the room as her mind worked to formulate some response, some appropriate reaction that would not get her immediately thrown out of his house.

"Forgive me." She struggled for words. "Dominic told me he worked out an arrangement with you. I assumed it was amicable."

"One does not have to be amicable to transfer property."

"I should go," Marguerite said quietly.

Julian did not disagree with her. He remained silent, his eyes narrowed on Eleni as Marguerite bowed slightly and backed out of the room. She shut the door to the study, leaving the two of them alone. Eleni stood trembling in her coat, not knowing what to say or do. He hadn't invited her to sit down. Had he already decided to send her away?

"I-I'm sorry," she stammered. "I don't know what to say."

Julian scoffed. "There is nothing to say. You have nowhere else to go," he stated bluntly. "And yet, when I was talking to my cousin, I got the distinct impression that you felt it beneath you to go to the home of a mal vampire."

She swallowed hard "I assure you that never once crossed my mind. Even if I'd had room for doubt, I know my brother-in-law wouldn't send me anywhere objectionable."

Julian's dark laughter made her skin prickle. "He sent you to me, and I'm entirely objectionable, ma chére." He raked his teeth across his lower lip, offering her a brief view of his fangs. "I have my own rules, and I couldn't care less what society thinks of me, or you, for that matter. What I do care about is the running of my household. I am the only master here, and I do not care for drama."

"Neither do I."

"Your history tells me otherwise. Now here you are, set to enter a mal vampire's household to try to preserve your rank. I suppose in some way you must think you're better than me, or that I am eternally stupid to take someone with an addiction into my house."

A lump had risen in her throat. "You're a vampire, I'm an Acolyte. I would never assume you to be of a lower rank than me."

A thin smile stretched his lips. "How modest you are."

She was ready to crack, ready to call Anya and Dominic and tell them she wanted to return to San Francisco. But, at the same time, she'd already brought tremendous shame on her family. She sighed. "I don't want my shame to reflect on my sister," she told him flatly. "I will do my part to fit in with your household. I only want to live in peace. I know immortality is permanently off limits to me, but I still have this life, and I just want to live...to be as happy as I can be with the time that I have. Surely, that's not too much to ask."

A mote of heat gleamed in his eyes for a fraction of a second. It was gone just as quickly. A trickle of unease flowed through her. Eleni was aware she'd somehow touched a nerve with him. Wary of her new Biter, she fell silent, and made a conscious decision to choose her words more carefully from now on. Better that, than give him more ammunition to hurt her with.

Confrontation stressed her out easily, a residual effect of Biter's Addiction. Even this brief conversation with him left Eleni's nerves frayed. Whatever she'd expected when she'd agreed to move to France, this was hardly the welcome she'd anticipated. Not only that, a dim throb nagged at her temples—a headache coming on. Julian Sévigné's intense scrutiny was almost unbearable. The sooner she made it to a private room, the better.

"Tell me about your life with my cousin, Dominic," he said, his shrewd expression a mask of curt impatience. "What role did you play in his household?"

"I stayed as Anya's guest. You know he no longer houses a harem? Not since he joined with my sister, Anya, in the blood bond," she said softly. "I believe they're happy." Or they would be now that they weren't babysitting her. "I had no formal role while living with them. I stayed in one of the guest suites, and they employed a series of doctors, Biters, and nurses to help me get well. Didn't Dominic tell you about all of that when you spoke to him?"

"We talked only briefly, a phone call. A few emails. Besides, I wanted to hear it from you."

"I can't imagine what Dominic must've said to convince you to take me in."

"He did nothing to convince me. I owe him my blood, and I believe that's why he called me. He knew you were a gift I could not refuse." Julian changed the subject. "Tell me, what did your sister think, you living in the same house as her husband?"

"I imagine there were times she thought…my presence was an inconvenience," she admitted, then shook her head. "Even so, I doubt that had anything to do with Dominic. He never sponsored me. Why would it bother her? He was never my Biter."

Julian squinted at her. "He never bit you? Not once?"

"Well, he…yes, but… it's hard to explain. My sister called him in to help me. I was grieving at the time, and—"

"With your addiction, you were beyond control?"

Her throat constricted. "Y-yes."

"I see. You lived isolated from him, then?"

"Not isolated, although I did have a suite of rooms to myself. As I said, I lived with them as my sister's guest."

He folded his hands on his desk and leaned forward in a gesture of unbending authority. "You will not be living as a guest in my house, let us make this much clear. Be aware, I was sent a letter of disclosure from the council regarding your condition. I'm well aware of the terms of your probation. You must prove that you can function as a lover and donor in a vampire household. Believe me when I say I will hold you to that. You are here for my pleasure, and from this moment forward, I expect you to take your duty seriously. Am I understood?"

She swallowed hard. "Completely."

"Good." He pushed his chair back, stood up, and walked around his desk. Frozen to the spot, she watched him cross the room to the door. An overwhelming sense of misery curled inside her. She stood back, even when he reached the door and held it open for her.

He scoffed. "You look like a frightened mouse. I'm not scheming to bite you. "

Eleni didn't doubt that. The way Julian swept his gaze over her gave her the impression he'd rather eat a bulb of raw garlic than sink his fangs into her throat.

Chapter Three

Julian walked Eleni through the house, pointing out hallways, opening doors to elegant, lamp lit rooms. "You may come and go from the house as you please, but tell someone where you are going. Henri is on call in the evenings. If there's somewhere you wish to travel during the day, you will have to make special arrangements."

He didn't stay in one place for longer than a moment.

At 5'11", she was by no means a short woman, but Julian was taller than her by at least three inches. His broad shoulders filled the doorway to the sitting room at the front of the house. He allowed her to wander through the room a moment to look around before he waved her back into the hallway. On her way through the door, her body brushed against his, and for a moment, their eyes met over the unexpected contact. Eleni's heartbeat accelerated. His body was warm and firm beneath the black sweater. She quickly looked away as heat blazed in her cheeks.

Without saying a word, he guided her across the grand foyer and through a swinging door to the kitchen.

"Claudette."

A reed-thin, gray-haired woman stood at the sink, filling up a silver tea kettle. Once she'd finished what she was doing and set the kettle on the stove, she bustled across the room while drying her hands with the folds of her white apron. She flicked her gaze over Eleni before glancing up at Julian in question. "*Monsieur…*"

"My new lover, Eleni Audridov."

"*Mademoiselle.*" Claudette nodded at her in a chilly greeting, and said in heavily accented English, "You would like some tea?"

"No, thank you. I'm fine."

The housekeeper murmured her acknowledgment, but before she could go back to her busywork, Julian called after her, "Claudette, do you know where I can find Gisele?"

"I'm here!" A young woman with a smoky voice bounded in through a side door carrying a basket of laundry on her hip. She was short and curvy, with warm brown eyes and a lion's mane of tawny hair. She set the laundry basket on a scarred kitchen table. "You needed me?"

Julian opened his mouth to speak, but his cell phone cut him off with a trilling ring. Muttering an oath, he took out his phone, looked at the number, then turned away from them before bringing the phone to his ear.

"Hallo?" He raked a hand through his hair and listened. He offered a curt reply in French, then lowered the phone from his ear and turned to Eleni. "I must take this call. Come to me at 3:00 AM sharp. I will be waiting in my office. For now, go with Giselle." He laid his hand against Eleni's lower back, urging her toward the young woman. Her skin tingled where his fingers splayed against her coat. Despite his tone of authority, his touch was surprisingly gentle.

"Giselle, show my new protégé to her room."

He didn't wait for an answer. He left the room talking into his cell, making apologies to the man on the phone. Through the doorway, Eleni watched him walk back in the direction of his office, leaving no doubt in her mind that he intended her to do as she was told.

"Never mind Julian," Gisele said minutes later as she led Eleni upstairs. "He's in rare form this evening. He usually doesn't hold onto his anger for very long."

"That's good to know."

"So, Julian told us you are from the United States. Is this your first time in France?"

Eleni shook her head. "I've been to Paris a few times—and Marseille. I've also vacationed in Nice."

Gisele gave her an incredulous look. "Did you expect the chateau to be like Nice?"

The comment embarrassed Eleni a little bit, but she played it off with a shrug. "I didn't know what to expect, honestly." She curled her hand around the rail and eyed Gisele's back. The woman reminded her of a young

Bridget Bardot with her curves and long, golden hair. She seemed nice, but not especially friendly. Eleni tried not to read too much into it. She had traveled to many countries where curt indifference was simply away of the culture, so she wasn't quite sure what to think at this point.

"You will be bored here with us, just so you know. Julian rarely goes out. He is…how you say?" She thought for a moment. "Reclusive?"

She tittered and waited for Eleni at the top of the stairs. They walked to the left of Saint Vincent's window, away from the balcony, and down a long hallway lined with closed doors.

"It's a shame Julian doesn't get out more," Giselle said wistfully. "He could do whatever he wanted—have fun, travel. He has a house in Paris, you know? He allowed me to stay there while I went to university. Claudette tells me he uses it when he's in the city on business, but I've never known him to go there. Like I said—a shame. He receives visitors here sometimes, but mostly he stays in his office and runs the vineyard behind closed doors. There is always the village, but not much goes on there. Certainly not like in the city."

Eleni liked the idea of that, being bored, left to her own devices. Secretly, she'd been hoping he wouldn't require her to attend social engagements, something she wasn't yet ready to face again even if it was part of her duty. It was too much pressure, being under that kind of scrutiny. She would find something to do with herself. Maybe pick up painting again, something she hadn't had the chance to do since college. Or maybe she'd try a new hobby. If Julian worked the way Gisele let on, she probably wouldn't see much of him anyway.

The windowless hallway was dimly lit with sconces along the burgundy-papered walls. It ran in a straight line past four pocket doors then turned a sharp left, creating an L shape. Along the attached wing, there were two more doors, and one at the very end on the opposite side of the hallway. Gisele led her there.

"This is it," Gisele said, and opened the door for her.

Eleni glanced into the suite and hesitated entering it. The room was elaborately appointed in the way of an elegant French home. There was a large bed, a dressing table and wardrobe, and a corner fireplace with gas logs. When at last she entered the room, an onrush of anxiety curled through her. Clearly the suite had been designed for a premiere protégé. It dawned on her that the rooms around the corner and down the hall must be the interconnected suites designed to house a harem. It amazed her. She knew this was the traditional design of a vampire harem, but she had never actually lived in a house arranged this way. Only the premiere would have a disconnected room such as this one.

Julian's suite would be at the opposite end of the hallway, in the opposing wing. A knot hung in her throat when she thought about that. Without a doubt, he planned to keep the traditional role in his house, regardless of her true status.

She entered the suite and noticed a private bathroom at the furthest end of the room. The door was open and she could see a claw foot tub with a gold spout, and a gold-rimmed mirror hanging on the wall. She turned and noticed her cases had been set in front of a mirrored closet door.

"Everything is to your liking?"

"Yes," she said, swallowing down the feeling of shock at being turned over to such an elegant room on her first day, and only moments after her first meeting with her new Biter. She trailed her hand over the bed drapes, cobalt blue velvet that hung like a sash from the wall behind the bed. Of course, it was not his fondness of her that made this happen. She knew better than that. She supposed it made sense he would put her here, since there were no other women in the house. She was his first, his premiere, by default.

"It's a lovely room, *non*? Julian chose everything specifically for you." While Eleni marveled over that interesting tidbit of information, Gisele swept her fingers over the top of the mahogany dresser and said, "I must admit it is exciting to have another woman in the house, someone my own age. It gets lonely here, you know? But now there is you." She smiled a small smile at Eleni's reflection in the dresser mirror. "I am sure we will become fast friends."

The words sent a tingling warning through her. *Stop it. You're being paranoid.*

"That would be nice," Eleni lied. She remembered Sabilla saying very much the same thing to her when Rubio had introduced her into the house. Their friendship had started out normal enough—sharing clothes, eating meals together. What a ruse that had been. At the very first opportunity, Sabilla had stabbed her in the back. It was nothing personal against Gisele. After all, Eleni had no idea how much Julian had told her, or any of the other members of his household staff about her past or her condition. The fact of the matter was simple. She never wanted to be close to anyone like that again—human or vampire.

Nevertheless, Gisele appeared pleased with her answer. She waited patiently while Eleni explored the suite.

The bedroom was large and open, with its own television tucked away in an entertainment armoire, and a small desk with an outlet to hook up her laptop computer. She walked toward the bathroom to peer inside. It was large, but not overwhelming. Her gaze skimmed over the vanity area with its bowl sink and a series of drawers for her cosmetics.

Looking back, Eleni had never met a more ruthless, driven Acolyte than Sabilla. It was unlikely Gisele could be as cold as that. Gisele was not even of the Acolyte class, so that alone meant their friendship could only extend so far. But Eleni had been burned once. She'd been a fool to trust Sabilla, and ultimately the woman's bold quest for immortality at any cost had not only been Rubio's downfall, but her own. She would never forget that.

Thinking about the past put her in a grim mood, when she should be counting herself lucky to have this second chance. Sabilla's treachery had not only cost the woman her status. For orchestrating such a cruel bid for power against her housemates, her bloodline had been cut from the Book of Acolytes. Sabilla's punishment might've seemed like poetic justice if not for the fact Eleni faced a similar sentence if she did not assimilate into Julian's household. The possibility of losing her identity within vampire society haunted her.

Who would she be if not an Acolyte? She came from a long line of distinguished Audridovs. Unease washed over her, and she tried to tamp it down. It did very little good to dwell in the past. Still, it weighed on her mind. Sabilla had taken risky chances that lured her to her fate. A woman of the serving class, like Gisele, didn't have so much to lose.

She went to the double closet doors and opened them. Inside, it was empty, except for a long fur coat. She ran her fingers through the thick gray fur, picked up the sleeve and nuzzled it against her cheek. Chinchilla. A gift from Julian? A frown etched her brow. It seemed strange that he'd leave her such an elaborate gift, when he seemed so resentful about taking her in.

From the closet doorway, Gisele asked, "Would you like me to unpack your cases for you? If you like, I can—"

"No, thank you. I can unpack everything myself."

Gisele seemed surprised. "Are you sure?"

"Yes, I'm positive." She forced a smile. "That way I will be able to find everything later without having to bother someone to help me search."

Something flicked through the maid's eyes, an emotion that passed too quickly for Eleni to read. She tossed back her honey blonde hair. "If that's your wish."

"Thank you," Eleni said, not meaning to sound so dismissive, but she was ready to be alone, to get her bearings. Already, she was thinking about where she'd set up her laptop. She was eager to send an email to Anya, let her know that she had arrived and was now in Julian's care.

She heard the door shut softly as Gisele left the room. Immediately, she felt as though a great weight had been lifted off her. Alone, standing in the massive closet, Eleni let out a breath of relief. This would, more than likely, be one of those rare chances she would have to be alone. Since she was the only protégé in the house, Julian might want her near him most of the time. He seemed serious and curt, and while he was attractive, the idea of sitting underfoot seemed intimidating and stressful.

Not only that, but her next probationary hearing was only months away. The idea of someone like Julian testifying about her wellbeing before the vampire council made her very uneasy. Not only was he a skeptical man, he didn't seem to like her very much. She drew a deep breath and left the closet, and began dragging her bags over to the bench at the foot of the bed. She had a feeling getting to know Julian would be a difficult task, but she had to make this arrangement work. Her future, and the future of the Audridov line, depended on it.

Chapter Four

Julian turned off his cell phone and dropped it onto his desk. Once again, his gaze strayed to the antique clock on the wall between the two bookcases. It was nearly 3:00 AM. He'd spent most of the night working, sorting through figures, making phone calls until twenty minutes earlier, when he'd taken a break and had gone upstairs to shower and change in preparation for his appointment with Eleni. After his shower, he'd dressed in a black satin bathrobe, and returned to his office to wait for her. Now that the night's work was finally behind him, he swiveled the chair away from his desk, and allowed himself a moment to relax.

His thoughts instantly drifted to his new protégé. It had been a very long time since a woman made him this restless. She'd walked into his office like a tall, blonde goddess, and his mouth had nearly dropped open. Her beauty had struck him like bolt of lightning. Wicked thoughts of taking her in all sorts of positions across his desk and in his bed had scattered his mind, and kept him distracted throughout the night. He should've shut down his computer and postponed all his calls until he'd had a chance to scratch his itch with her, but he had investors to think about. Business couldn't wait. Still, all night he'd watched the clock, anticipating the hour when she would come to his office and he could sample her sweetness. It wouldn't be long now, mere minutes.

When Dominic had asked him to take in an Acolyte fallen into disgrace, he had initially refused. He could only imagine what strife that would bring to his peaceful household. But, of all his relatives, Dominic was the one who stayed in touch with him the most and annoyed him the least. When his cousin had explained the young woman was his bloodmate's younger sister, Julian had reluctantly agreed to shelter her as a favor to both Dominic and his new vampiress.

Eleni was not at all what he had expected. When she'd stepped into his office looking like a lost lamb, her pale blue eyes resting on his face, an instant heated attraction had soared through him. It had also angered him. Of course, the one Acolyte he'd agree to take into his home would have to be striking, with the features of a living Venus—her beauty incongruent to his monstrous scars.

Brooding over this, he went to the mini bar, and pulled out a chilled bottle of Sévigné wine. He shouldn't have been so harsh with her. The deal had been made before her arrival. And he couldn't say he was displeased with her. That was far from the truth. He had never seen a more attractive Acolyte. A tall, slender body to offer him pleasure, full lips for sucking him to ecstasy. If she had been born two hundred years ago, there would have been sonnets written in her honor of her ethereal beauty. Vampires would have lined up with trinkets to entice her into accepting their sponsorship. With the right selection, she would have been immortal not long after her debut into society. But that was not the case. She was a modern woman, and now, she was his. He fully intended to show her the pleasurable benefits of living under his roof.

Apparently, she was well aware of her poor state. He had not missed the sadness in her eyes, and something in that had touched him. He understood sadness. He'd lived through lifetimes of it. And he could not fathom how such a lovely creature could have been so ill used. The vampire who mistreated her was a fool.

He wanted to run his hands through her pale hair, feel the cool silk flow through his fingers. Her mouth was round and plump and completely fascinating. He wondered how it would look with her kneeling before him with his cock sliding between those cherry red lips. He intended to find out.

A light rap on the door, he looked up. Already his cock stirred to semi-hardness.

"Enter," he commanded, and settled back, expecting, anticipating Eleni. He didn't realize how much he wanted to see her, to simply look at her again, to attempt to unravel the mysteries of his new protégé, until the left side door opened, and Gisele stepped through. A wave of disappointment flowed through him when she entered the room and closed the door.

Her hands hidden behind her, she stood there wide-eyed, like a child with a secret. A thin smile curved his mouth as he reached beneath the bar for a corkscrew. "You helped my new protégé settle into her room?"

"I showed her the room. I assume she is still upstairs unpacking."

He looked up, fixed his eyes piercingly on her face. "*She* is unpacking?"

Gisele froze. "It was her decision. I offered, but she declined."

Interesting. Gisele often left Claudette to take up her chores. The housekeeper was getting older, and he feared the day he would lose her. She had been a trusted servant to him for many years. He would have to bring Eloise from Paris if something happened to Claudette, and that was far from ideal as Eloise was not getting any younger herself. He didn't know how the woman would handle moving from the city to the chateau, but on the other hand, he didn't think Gisele wouldn't be able to handle running his house.

His brow furrowed. For the past few years, he had been wondering what to do with Gisele. She was a woman now, twenty-four, probably not many years younger than Eleni. Still, he would always think of her as a child, as she was Claudette's great niece, and he had watched her grow up in his home. Whenever he looked at her, he couldn't help seeing the bright-eyed little girl Claudette had begged him to take in, but it seemed like Gisele should be doing something more with her life. Discovering her passions or putting her degree in literature to good use. He knew Claudette was certainly worried about it.

After a long moment of silence, Gisele leaned her head against the door and said, "Eleni is beautiful. Elegant."

Julian could certainly agree with that. "Her breeding is evident."

"I suppose." Gisele frowned faintly and pushed away from the door. She crossed the room and came to stand at the edge of the bar while he uncorked the bottle of wine. "Still, I thought she would be...I don't know. More sophisticated?"

He chuckled. "You thought she would be French."

Instead of laughing with him, a frown creased her brow. Julian sensed an undercurrent of tension, as though Gisele perhaps wanted to tell him something, but didn't know how. Perhaps Eleni had seemed dismissive to the girl. Gisele was not used to being treated that way. She had been raised to treat Chateau du Sévigné as though it were her own home. In a way, it was, even though she was still a servant.

"What's on your mind?" he asked.

She started to speak, but hesitated. Julian frowned. Something about the curious look on her face made him think she was about to say something important, but before she uttered a word, she stopped herself, her lips pressing together in a thin line. She shook her head. "It's nothing. You're working."

"I was, but not now. It's too hard to concentrate." He didn't tell her it was because he couldn't stop thinking about his new protégé. He couldn't keep his thoughts off her body, and his desire to sample the sweetness of her blood.

"You know," he said as he poured wine—a glass for Gisele, a glass for himself. "Ms. Audridov—Eleni—has gone through a lot. On top of that, she is American. It may take her time to acclimate herself to our ways, so be a friend to her."

"Of course," she said as she took the wineglass and brought it to her lips. Her dark eyes watched him across the rim of the glass as she sipped.

He took his glass and returned to his desk. Once again, his gaze strayed to the clock. It was a few minutes after the hour. He frowned. Perhaps Eleni intended to be fashionably late.

"I'm going to take this with me." Gisele held her glass up as if to toast her departure.

Julian saluted her with his glass, and the minute she was out of the room, he opened his computer and tapped into the security camera feed to look for Eleni.

It seemed ridiculous to be so nervous. After all, by moving into his house it was as if they had a signed contract to be free with one another. Still, Eleni felt awkward and tense as she walked down the stairs to the main foyer. She'd kept a careful eye on the time, but after her shower she'd hesitated over everything—how to arrange her hair, and what dress to wear for her evening with Julian.

Her own inefficiency frustrated her. At one time, she'd known by instinct what to wear for a lover. It had seemed almost second nature to her, and only during special occasions had she given her appearance any real thought. But her earlier meeting with Julian left her feeling nervous and unsure of herself. It didn't help that he was drop dead gorgeous, either. She was used to seeing judgment in other people's eyes and hadn't expected anything different from him, but it was more than that. Even though he had accepted her into his house, he didn't seem the least bit charmed with her. The idea bothered her more than she cared to admit.

At the last minute, she'd fastened her long straight hair into a simple coil at the nape of her neck and decided to wear the red, body skimming halter dress her sister had given her as a reward for her success in going six months without being bitten. Perhaps in some way, the dress would give her strength, because she certainly needed courage.

The silence of the house made her hyper-aware of the way her red suede heels clicked over the marble floors. The solitary echo reminded her of the many times she'd visited her mother's mausoleum. Anya had gone with her only once. All the other times, through years of visitation, Eleni had gone alone, and the marble corridors had been devoid of everything but the haunting sound of her own footfalls.

The last time she'd gone to leave flowers for her mother, she'd been living with Rubio for about a year. She'd rarely known a moment's peace in his house. The rooms there were always occupied, the halls ringing with the busy chatter of the other Acolytes in his harem. It had annoyed her at first, but after so many months, she'd grown used to having that noise around her.

While facing her mother's name engraved in stone, she'd stood in that bubble of absolute silence and realized that as much as she missed Ekaterina Audridov's guidance, she didn't belong there. The mausoleum was no place for the living. It was a place for ghosts.

Chateau du Sévigné gave her much that same feeling.

Avoiding the watchful eyes of St. Vincent, she entered the hallway beneath the second floor balcony, and was on her way to Julian's office when one of the double doors opened. Eleni stopped short. It must be Julian coming to look for her, she thought, but to her surprise, Gisele stepped out of the room carrying a glass of red wine.

The scene struck Eleni like a bolt out of the past. She took a step back, but there was nowhere to go. It was too late to hide. Gisele shut the door softly, and as she turned her direction, their eyes met, and Gisele jumped slightly.

"*Mon dieu!*" Gisele's hand fluttered in surprise. She laid it against her heart and laughed in relief. "Eleni, but you gave me a fright."

A slow heat crept into her face. "I have an appointment with Julian," she said dully, unable to take her eyes off Gisele's wine glass.

"Never mind me." Gisele took a sip of wine and as she passed Eleni in the hall. "Go on in. He should be ready to see you now."

The servant's stiletto boot heels rang through the long corridor. Eleni hadn't considered Julian might be in his office with someone else. Her confidence shaken, she watched Gisele walk away, her curls bouncing against her back, until she passed through the archway at the far end of the hall and veered off to the right in the direction of the kitchens.

A strong sense of disappointment rose in her, and she struggled to tamp it down. If Gisele was Julian's lover, it was no business of hers. But, at the same time, it bothered her. Although she didn't know Julian well, one of the supposed benefits of living with him was that he didn't keep a harem. It never occurred to her she might be placed in competition with someone on his serving staff. She had always thought such a thing was taboo.

In spite of her mixed feelings, she went over to the door and knocked. She heard shuffling within the room, and a moment later, the door opened and Julian stood there in a black bathrobe, looking severe and disheveled. He raked his eyes over her from head to toe then pushed the door wider to allow her entrance.

"I wondered how long you would stand in my hallway."

"I saw Gisele," she said as she brushed past him and glanced around the study. "I thought you might be…indisposed."

He shut the door and turned to her. "Gisele is a servant, and I respect that position."

She nodded, averting her eyes. Despite the awkwardness of the conversation, she was relieved to hear it from Julian's own mouth. Still, she had seen no evidence of a blood source. Who wouldn't naturally assume that he might use someone young and pretty like Gisele to feed from?

"Care to sit down?" He gestured toward a small seating area in front of the fireplace.

She walked over to one of the chocolate leather wingchairs and sat in it, the seat cool against the backs of her legs. Julian had gone to the wet bar in the corner and looked perfectly at ease—if a little distracted. He set his empty glass down on the counter, and pulled out a second stemmed glass from beneath the bar.

"You're in luck," he said, ice rattling as he pulled the bottle of wine from the bucket and began to pour. "I was just sampling this new vintage of Sévigné red we hope to export next year. Perhaps you will like it."

The wine. Gisele. A flood of relief poured through her, even if she was only putting two and two together.

He nestled the bottle back into the ice, then scooped up the glasses one by one, and carried them over to where she was sitting. Instead of offering her the wine right away, he towered there, looking down at her. Did he expect her to reach out and take the glass without him offering it to her first? Perhaps he played a game, or this was some unspoken test. Eleni looked at the wine glass, then up at him. His gray eyes glittered with some fierce, indefinable emotion that awakened a sweet fluttering low in her belly. "Is something the matter?" she asked him.

He didn't answer her. A faint smile tugged at his lips, giving him a smug appearance. At last, he held out the wine, and it seemed almost as if he dared her to take it. His hand was cupped beneath the bowl, the stem caught between his fingers.

Eleni shifted uncomfortably in her seat. There was something remotely intimate about the presentation. Nevertheless, she accepted the glass, pinching it by the stem. His fingers grazed hers, work roughened and surprisingly warm.

"Thank you." Her voice trembled a little, but if Julian noticed, he said nothing.

He backed away, and as he sat down in the chair across from her, he lifted his glass. "For our courage."

She could certainly relate to the toast. She raised her glass, and when he took a drink, she did the same. The wine tasted sweet. It was flavored strongly of blackcurrant. The tannin made her mouth instantly dry, but she was already so nervous it hardly mattered. Julian swirled the wine in his glass a moment, steely eyed and thoughtful looking, then he leaned forward and set his glass on the sofa table. Eleni's heart fluttered. The moment to prove herself to him had finally come.

Splayed across the chair in rakish fashion, he traced his thumb over his lower lip and took a deep breath. "I think you know what this evening means."

"I do."

"When was the last time you were bitten?"

Eleni swallowed hard. "It's been over a year."

"Do you crave it?"

"Sometimes." She swallowed hard and stared into the flames for a moment. "But the craving is nothing like it once was."

He watched her steadily, heightening the tension that twisted inside her. "Get up."

Her head snapped up in alarm. The curt tone of his voice made her heart race. But she saw no evidence of anger on his face or in his posture. Lust burned bright in his eyes. He gazed toward her neck, then to her breasts.

"Reveal yourself to me."

She took another sip of wine, then rose from the chair and set the glass down on the sofa table. Her mind whirred as her nervousness intensified. Had she really come this far after her fall? Until now she'd gone untested. It worried her that she might not be able to please him. She questioned her endurance, and her ability to fall into the role of a lover again, but at the same time, she wanted him. She wanted to test herself. She may not be worthy of love, but wanted to feel something—sex, pleasure, the sweet pain of fangs sinking into her throat.

Reaching back, she unfastened the top of her halter dress, her hands shaking as she lowered the straps, revealing her breasts to him. Her nipples peaked to hard nubs, and his eyes darkened. Close-mouthed, he ran his tongue over his fangs, and a shiver passed through her. A sudden ache throbbed between her thighs.

His thumb stroked over his lips, and she could have sworn she felt it deep inside her, a physical caress. His eyes drifted to the lower half of the dress, still tight around her thighs.

"Show me more."

Chapter Five

Julian watched in aroused awe as Eleni did as he commanded. Her shy obedience made his cock surge to attention. He knew she was no innocent—Dominic had told him her entire story. He had read every page of her probationary records from the Vampire Council. And yet, she was not at all what he expected from those reports.

There was a vulnerability about her that drew him. Nervousness was written all over her face, but a high flush of arousal also clung there, and this pleased him very much. Nothing would please him more than watching her beautiful face while she came for him again and again.

Their relationship might be strained, but he wanted her to desire him.

The lower half of the dress had a back zipper. She reached for it with both hands, one to slide the zipper down, the other to hold the fabric, and Julian's eyes zeroed in on the thrust of her breasts.

"That position suits you," he told her. "I must remember it."

The zipper gave, and she gently worked the fitted dress over her slender hips. The fabric whispered to the floor and became a puddle of crimson at her feet. She stepped out of it, her towering red heels and matching thong accentuating her mile high legs.

"Take down your hair."

She reached for the pins and pulled them free. Her hair gleamed like moonlight as it uncoiled and tumbled down her shoulders. *Mon dieu*, but she was a beautiful woman. He had been around many lovely women in his lifetime, but he had never met one like her. Every curve of her enticed him. She dropped the pins onto the fallen gown, and waited for his next command.

He held out his hand, and she sauntered over to him. He could not take much more of her visual teasing. He gripped her wrist, tugged her closer so she had to straddle him on the chair. Her burgundy thong was sheer with a lace edge, and spaghetti straps that rode high on her hips. He ached to taste her succulent breasts, and so he did. He sipped and kneaded, caressed and squeezed. Her soft sighs urged him to tease the tender peaks with flicks of his tongue.

He shifted, moved her off his lap, and encouraged her to go down on her knees in front of him. Eleni consented. The soft fur of the rug cushioned her knees. While she situated herself, Julian untied the belt of his black robe. His skin was dark, peppered lightly with black hair. A treasure trail led down his taut abdomen to his cock, which lay semi-hard. His hands bunched in her hair, when she blew along his shaft, making the taut muscles of his stomach twitch in response.

"Take me into your mouth," he commanded in a voice roughened with desire.

Her eyes on his, she smoothed her hands up his thighs, her manicured nails raking over his flesh. She gripped him in her hands, levered him toward her, and with her eyes locked on his, she rubbed the head of his cock over her lips before she drew him into her mouth.

Julian took a deep breath, spread his legs more to accommodate her, and urged her to continue sucking him. Every stroke of her tongue, every glide of her lips, licked through his body like fire. Her hands rubbed and explored, cupping the taut sac of his balls. She licked her way down the shaft to suckle him there, first one side, then the other, while he writhed on the chair, trying very hard not to show the extent of his pleasure. She took him into her mouth again and took him deep. Her fingers slick from her saliva, she trailed them down his sac, massaged the swatch of skin between his balls and his anus before entering him.

A growl purred from his throat. His eyes opened a fraction, black, hot, watching her continue her ministrations while delving her fingers into his ass. She stroked him, finger fucking him, rubbing him inside while she sucked him ever closer to an orgasm. She tasted the salt of his pre-come, felt him bear down harder on her fingers. A strong hand caught in her hair urged her to take him deeper. Her lips were burning, raw, and a tense desire had begun to grow inside her, high and sweet. Her clit was hard, her inner thighs slick with her own passion. She wished his cock was pounding into her, taking her hard, without mercy, until she had no other choice but to let go of all her pent up anxiety.

Julian leaned his head back, watching her fuck him with her mouth. His hands stroked her hair, his hips pumped in small motions. His hand rested on the back of her head in a gesture of praise and encouragement. Turned on by the heated look in his eyes, she laved her tongue around the crown of his cock and raked her nails along his corded thighs. Soon, he was lost to the motion. Ecstasy blazed through him, sweet and high, a thousand delicious sensations coaxed forward by those plush, red lips. As his control began to slip away, he serenaded her with his ragged, uneven breathing.

"Ah, yes…" he growled, then stiffened and fell into a tense silence as he reached climax. He came in thick spurts against her tongue and was left shaking, gasping for breath.

A low moan rumbled in his chest. His expression hazy, he watched her lick every drop of him. In reward for a job well done, he stroked her cheek, his fingers trailing a path to her chin, which he lifted so that she looked up at him, her chest rising and falling fast with her panting breaths. "You've pleased me, well, *tyros.*"

Tyros. Unsponsored one. The name struck her like a knife to the heart. He let go of her chin, and she sat back on her knees, realizing she still had her high heels on. While he recovered in the chair, she turned around to go pick up her clothes. She trembled with lust, her clit throbbing, begging for attention. She wished he would bend her over the sofa table and fuck her from behind, but it was too soon after her arrival. She couldn't make demands of him now. Instead, she reached for her dress.

"Leave it." The command stopped her cold. His eyes watched her like a viper. The robe fell open when he stood up, and she drank in the sight of his lean, chiseled body. "We are not done yet." He walked around her and across the room to a gold metal screen covering the wall to the right of the fireplace. He touched a switch she hadn't even noticed was there, and the gilt screen slid aside. It was the door to an elevator. If he hadn't shown her, she'd never have known it was there.

"Come on. Get up."

She did as he said. "My clothes…"

"You don't need them."

He expected her to walk through the house wearing nothing but high heels? She glanced at the discarded dress and was about to make a grab for it anyway when he called her down.

"Eleni," his voice was stern, "I haven't fucked you yet and I'm becoming impatient."

Was he trying to make her uncomfortable on purpose? She didn't want to question his motives, but Rubio had gone out of his way to put her in more uncomfortable scenarios than she cared to remember. And he had done so out of spite. She sincerely hoped that wasn't one of Julian's secret kinks.

Feeling exposed and a little awkward, she braced her hand on the side of the leather chair to help pull herself to her feet. As hard as it was for her to trust him, she had no real choice but to give her new Biter the benefit of the doubt.

Julian stood aside to let her into the narrow elevator. When she was inside with him, he slid the grate closed and pressed the button to take them upstairs. As soon as they were in motion, he turned to her and pulled her close to him. Ah, to feel a woman in his arms again, one that was his for the taking, not a borrowed vein from Marguerite's harem. He found her mouth and kissed her, nipping those full sweet lips still salty from his essence. The warm satin of her skin enticed him to slide his hands along hips and around to the smooth mounds of her buttocks. He pulled her taut against him, flesh to flesh, and nearly groaned. He traced his tongue along her throat, amusement curling through him when she stiffened ever so slightly at the gentle scrape of his fangs.

Looking down between them, he ran his finger beneath the side strap of her thong. "This is the sexiest thing I've ever seen." Her stomach muscles tensed when he traced his fingers over the sheer fabric, his middle finger sliding soft as a whisper along her moist slit.

"Does that feel good for you?"

"Yes," she said, breathing in sharply when he repeated the action once more before he slipped his fingers beneath the lace edge of her panties and stroked his way through her folds to find her clit.

Eleni clutched at his shoulders as if hanging on for dear life. Her hands bunched in the fabric of his satin robe while she ground herself against his sure fingers.

She was vaguely aware that the elevator had stopped. But she didn't care. His mouth was on hers, his hands driving her toward sweet oblivion. Their breathing mingled together in a harsh symphony.

"Oh…" She leaned her head back, heart galloping, frustration driving her toward orgasm. She was so close, so close to coming, the rise of desperation in her blood, needing only a little more to push her over the edge. Instead of giving her the release she craved, he withdrew his fingers, kissed her throat, and stepped back.

"Julian!" she panted, the air cool against her bare skin without his body shielding her. "You…Julian, please…"

"Not yet," he said, and she felt herself growing peevish with him.

"You're a tease…" she chastised him, breathless.

To her surprise, he chuckled, a deep, rich sound that danced over her skin and sent a small thrill spiraling straight to her core. Gone was the man who had seemed so angry with her when she had first arrived.

"Do you want me to fuck you in the elevator?" The opposite door had already slid open, revealing a long hallway. He reached out and pushed back the gold grate that barred them inside and gestured down the hall to a set of carved double doors. "My room is just there." Taking her by the hand, he lured her from the elevator, pulling her up close against his body. "I'd much rather see you naked and panting while splayed across my bed."

She almost moaned aloud at the mental picture he created with those words. His eyes darkened with a promise of pleasure. Eleni nodded quietly, allowing him to guide her from the elevator and along the shadowy corridor in the direction of the master suite.

A minute later, their bodies tangled together, touching, kissing, caressing, they stumbled through the doorway into Julian's room. Someone had come up before them to prepare the suite for them. The fireplace blazed, sending orange light high across the dark blue wallpaper, illuminating an antique armoire and a massive four poster bed arranged along the wall facing the fire. Shadows danced in the corners, over sullen tapestries and flowing blue drapes.

Julian bumped the door shut with his knee, and guided Eleni back through the windowless room to the bed. With quick, questing fingers she tried to push the robe back over his shoulders, but his arms were caught in the sleeves, and he made no move to let her slip the garment from his body. No matter, she trailed her hands over his chest and down to his taut abs, reveling in the feel of his muscles jerking at her touch. She couldn't keep her hands off him.

The cold satin comforter touched the back of her legs and she shivered. Julian's gaze zeroed in on her nipples as they peaked, and he leaned forward to flick his tongue over one taut bud then the other.

A ripple of pleasure cascaded through her, and she threw her blonde head back and sighed. Julian growled under his breath, and leaned forward to lick her from throat to chin.

"Are you offering your blood to me, *mon amour*?"

"I'm yours to take. All of me," she whispered, her body so hot she thought she might burn to cinders if he didn't fuck her soon.

Whatever game he played with her, she was no match for it. He seemed to be able to turn his emotions on and off with a switch. First he hated her, now he made her feel beautiful and desirable. She had assumed he would dismiss her after he'd exerted his dominance over her downstairs. Instead, he caressed her breasts, her hips, and thighs, at last turning her around and pushing her down onto the cool mattress so that her ass pointed up into the air.

"Such a perfect view," he said, the words rumbling low in his chest. He kissed the right cheek, then the left, nipping playfully with his teeth. Then he began to tug at his robe, and at first she thought he intended to strip it off, but all he did was remove the fabric sash.

"What are you doing?" she asked.

"Put your hands behind your back."

Her heart thumped harder, faster. She did as she was told, and he wound the strip of satin around her wrists, binding them together. She turned her head to the side to try to get a glimpse of him, but he was too far out of her field of vision. He struck her ass cheek sharply for her efforts, and she stiffened in surprise.

Another growl rumbled from him. "I didn't give you permission to look at me."

Despite his fierce tone, he rubbed her stinging flesh with the soothing palm of his hand.

"Sweet Eleni, I'm going to enjoy fucking you," he said, his voice a deep rumble of need. "Just the sight of you makes my cock hard. Tell me, is that what you want? Your vampire master to fuck you? Tell me how much you want it."

Eleni swallowed hard, struggling for words. She did want it. More than she cared to admit. Her answer didn't come fast enough, and he struck her tender buttocks again and again, making her cry out in little mewling notes.

"I didn't hear you. How much do you want me?"

"More," she gasped when his massaging hands stroked and soothed her heated bottom, "more than anything."

Her answer must've pleased him. The bed dipped as he shifted his weight, moving so he could drag the straps of her thong down her thighs. He left her panties halfway down, so that the fabric stretched taut between her parted knees. Cool air brushed against the hot wetness of her pussy, and in those brief moments, he didn't touch her. The lack of his hands on her made her feel empty and alone. She moaned, needing him to fill her, to give her some kind of release. "Please, Julian...more."

He massaged her inner thighs in slow circles with his thumbs, moving higher with each pleasurable movement, until she was dizzy with need. Aching for fulfillment, she moaned a little as he approached her inner thighs and lingered there, rubbing, teasing her, the tips of his fingers faintly grazing her swollen nether lips. It was sheer torture, the way her pussy throbbed for him.

At last, he slid a finger into her, probing deep, where she needed him most. A breathy shudder racked her body at the high, hot feelings that flashed through her.

"Good, is it? You're so wet for me," he commented breathily. "I wager I could make you come with a few strokes like this."

Her heart beat faster as his fingers explored her moist slit, spearing through her pussy lips to find her swollen clit. He massaged it in sweet, small circles that felt so good it sent a surge of blood throbbing in her temples, the sound a heady drumbeat in her ears. She rubbed herself against his strong fingers in desperation. She was so close to coming, poised right there on the edge, aching for it, needing to come, anything to release her from this carnal spell.

Eleni whimpered when his fingers left her body. He had pulled back to remove his robe.

Her eyes drifted shut, her body tense, her upper lip beaded with cool sweat while she waited for him to mount her from behind. At once, his hand was on her back, urging her to tilt her hips. Trembling, she complied. He spoke guttural words she could barely make out, but the fact that he was driven to swear in her name aroused her all the more.

Behind her, he nudged his cock against her slick opening, and she wiggled back toward him, urging him to take her. Eleni cried out in bliss when he thrust into her hard, just the way she hoped he would.

"Ah, yes," he hissed, on a sharp intake of breath. Her inner walls clutched at him, and in response, he groaned loudly, his hands biting into her hips. He began to ride her in long, slow strokes.

The hot, rhythmic penetration was all she could take. The moment Julian reached around her to rub her clitoris, she shivered as sweet release flowed through her in a heated rush, breaking down all her defenses, launching her into a mad spiral of pleasure.

Goosebumps peppered her flesh as she came, her body convulsing in rapture.

"That's it. Come for me," he murmured against her shoulder, kissing her there, scraping her with his teeth as his stabbing thrusts grew harder, more frantic.

Ripe fear curled through her. Her whole body tensed in anticipation of his bite. Julian uttered what sounded like an erotic obscenity then sank his fangs into her shoulder.

Never before had it felt as heady or potent as this. His fangs lit her up like liquid fire. Pure lust blazed through her veins. Her nerves sang with minute vibrations, and colored light pulsed behind her closed eyelids. Her lips formed an O as she fought for breath. In an instant, her entire body tensed and released, a second, blinding orgasm flared through her, growing brighter and more intense until her thoughts scattered into shivering, pulsating oblivion.

They collapsed together on the bed, their panting breaths mingling together. Julian released her, his tongue swiping over the tingling bite wounds before planting a quick kiss on the back of her neck. He rolled off her, and stretched out alongside her on the mattress.

After a moment, Julian eased up on his elbow and released the binding around her wrists. Having her arms free again was blessed relief. Eleni's muscles burned from being in one position for so long, something she hadn't noticed until now.

She turned over onto her back and rubbed her wrists, grateful for the cool air that brushed against her overheated skin. Beside her, Julian rested with his arm flung over his eyes. The skin from just above his elbow was a weathered brown, the color of distressed leather. The sight of it startled her. Not because the scars were gruesome, or that she hadn't known he'd been burned a long time ago, but because the wounds weren't imagined. They were real, and somehow that seemed impossible. Julian had such a dominant personality, it seemed as though he should be immune to physical harm.

The burn scars chased up his arm, and along his left side. She couldn't see much more than that, but she guessed the withered discolorations must cover most, if not all, of his back. It made sense now why he hadn't wanted to remove his clothes for her—the scars bothered him. He obviously hadn't wanted her to see them on their first night together.

Eleni gave herself a mental shake. The last thing she wanted was to seem disrespectful, or to upset him by staring. Worst of all, he might conclude that the burns could in some way affect her ability to bond with him.

Julian's breathing had grown deep and regular. Perhaps it was for the best that he slept. Feeling awkward, she sat up on the edge of the bed and looked around for something to wear. If she remembered right, her room was straight down the hallway, past the balcony overlooking the front foyer, and at the end of the opposing corridor. Surely, she could find her way there on her own.

There was nothing nearby save for Julian's black robe still draped across the end of the bed. She eased off the mattress and grabbed it, then flipped the robe around her shoulders. It was far too large. The hem touched the top of her feet.

She held the robe pinched together and searched the floor for the belt. Julian had discarded it, but she wasn't exactly sure where. When she looked across the bed and saw him sitting up on his elbow watching her, she startled.

"Where are you going?" he asked.

"I was going to return to my room."

"No." Julian threw back the sheets, and was out of bed in an instant.

Her heart leapt when he prowled toward her. He grabbed the front of the robe by the lapels and stripped it back over her shoulders so that it slid easily from her body onto the floor. Julian snatched it up and balled it into a wad of fabric before tossing it into the corner of the room.

Eleni opened her mouth to explain, but Julian cut her short when he swept her off her feet and carried her back to bed. "If it were my wish to dismiss you to your room, I would do so," he said as he returned her to the mattress. "But this is our first daylight together. You will sleep here with me."

Chapter Six

Eleni woke feeling sluggish and hazy brained. Disoriented, she stared at the gentleman's chair along the shadowy wall by the bed, and when she noticed the black sash tossed across the bentwood arm, she remembered Julian's touch, his heated kisses. She propped herself up on her elbow and looked around, noting that a fire still burned in the gas fireplace. She shoved her hair back from her face, wondering what time it was.

Julian slept beside her, pale and silent, the black satin sheets pooled around his waist. At the sight of his muscular chest, her heart did a somersault. One night with him, and already he had given her so much pleasure.

Her gaze lingered on his ripped abs, and the dark trail of hair that disappeared beneath the covers. Reaching back, she laid a hand on his muscular chest. His skin felt cool, and his breathing was so shallow one might think he was not breathing at all. Not wanting to wake him, she withdrew her hand, and contented herself with staring at him.

All her life she'd been around handsome men, but Julian's dark good looks made her weak inside. In awe of him, she trailed her gaze along his chiseled jaw, dark with a day's growth of beard stubble. His shiny black hair fanned out across the pillow, beckoning her touch.

He slept with his hand behind his head and tucked beneath the pillows, the unguarded pose exposing the burn scars along his left side. Even if she hadn't known about his scars before her arrival, it wouldn't have mattered to her that they were there. They didn't seem to pain him, and they didn't detract at all from his raw male beauty.

Of course, a vampire's ideal beauty differed from a human's perspective. Eleni had been taught that vampires prized perfection from the time she was old enough to understand what her role in life would be. For vampires, their bodies had to last them through hundreds, and in rare cases, thousands, of years. Preservation of their looks was important to them, and they prized in themselves the same kind of flawless beauty they looked for in a bloodmate.

To Julian, his scars must seem like unforgivable flaws. A needless shame, in her opinion, but at least now she could begin to understand why he sent away his entire harem.

She was grateful he had made an exception for her, even if he had only accepted her because she was a blood gift from Dominic. However, that didn't mean she was foolish enough to surrender her heart to Julian. There were two sides to people. She had learned that lesson the hard way. Eleni stared at her new Biter a moment longer, then pulled back the sheets and climbed out of bed.

She wrapped herself in a satin sheet that had fallen off the bed during the day, and padded quietly across the room to the door.

Out in the hallway, she walked toward the open balcony overlooking the grand entrance. A faint glow clung to the stained glass window of St. Vincent, the gemstone colors radiant in the dying light of day. She passed in front of it, looking down over the silent entryway as she crossed into the west wing of the house. Walking past the empty silence of so many uninhabited rooms disturbed her. A house of this size was not meant to be empty. The lack of laughter and idle chatter made the chateau seem less like a place for the living, and more like a mausoleum.

A chill passed over her when at last she turned the corner. Trying to ignore the empty row of adjoined rooms, Eleni fixed her eyes on the double doors to the suite Julian had set aside for her. Even then, she couldn't quell the sense of oppressive loneliness and an almost queasy sense of fear. The silence and stillness made the hall seem almost haunted—with what, she couldn't guess. Not ghosts, she was certain of that, but perhaps centuries of bad memories had left an impression.

Eleni reached the double doors, and grabbed for the handle. She entered the room without a second thought, and yelped in surprise at the sight of a woman standing in front of her closet door in a bright blue dress.

It seemed as though the world stopped for an instant. Her attention settled on the open-mouthed expression of shock on Gisele's face. The servant stood amid a mess of strewn clothes.

Eleni could barely believe what she was seeing. The maid had dressed herself in the sleek blue evening dress she'd brought with her from San Francisco. It was ill-fitting on Gisele's body shape. It fit her trim waist perfectly, but fit too tight across her large bust and curvy hips.

A sharp pain lanced Eleni's heart. Anya had given her the dress as a sobriety gift before she'd left for France. But Gisele hadn't stopped with just the dress. She wore a slash of red lipstick that Eleni suspected came from her makeup drawer in the bathroom. But what infuriated her most, was that the servant had secured her lush, honey blonde hair into a loose knot at the nape of her neck with her great grandmother's floral hairpins.

Gisele's face blazed scarlet. "I came in to prepare the room for you, and the dress—"

"—was on the bed," Eleni cut her off in a flat voice. "Yes, I know where I left it."

"Is it truly a reason to be angry?" Gisele asked in stiff defense. Shaken, she looked remarkably like a little girl discovered playing in her mother's wardrobe.

"I don't know what to think," Eleni said truthfully. She pulled Julian's bed sheet tighter around her, clinging to it like a shield. "We both know you shouldn't be in here going through my things."

Before her date with Julian, she'd tried on the dress, but decided it was too long, too glamorous for the evening. She'd left it lying across the foot of the bed with the intention of hanging it up later. She didn't know how to take the situation—as an insult, or an awful gesture of flattery? Gisele was a veritable stranger. One she would have to live with, but a stranger all the same. It felt like a violation of more than simply trust.

"Take it off." Even to her own ears, her voice sounded angry and resolute. She had lived in Rubio's house with eighteen other women, and while it had ended poorly, no one had ever trespassed on her privacy in this way. No one had ever worn her clothes or jewelry without asking her for permission first.

Gisele began to shimmy out of the too-tight dress. "You plan to tell Julian." It sounded like an accusation.

The thought hadn't crossed her mind until now. It didn't surprise her that Gisele would be worried, but Eleni didn't need to involve him in a small squabble she could handle by herself. If she presented Julian with a problem so soon after moving in, he might believe her to be a troublemaker.

She turned her back while Gisele changed, but now that Eleni knew she could not trust the woman, it was hard not to watch her in the dresser mirror. Eleni glimpsed Gisele's white bra straps as the servant turned to toss the dress onto the end of the bed. She spoke to her reflection.

"I will clean my own room from this day forward, is that understood?"

"Perfectly," Gisele responded stiffly. Once she had pulled on her jeans, she slipped her feet into a pair of gray flats and grabbed for her yellow patchwork cardigan off the floor. She whipped the sweater around her shoulders like a cape, and had only pulled one arm through before she started toward the bedroom door.

"My grandmother's hairpins, too," Eleni called after her.

Gisele froze, backtracked. Making no move to look Eleni in the eye, she stepped over to the dresser and fumbled to remove the delicate, enameled flowers. Her hands were shaking as she pulled the pins free and scattered them on top of the dresser. At once, she turned on her heel and hurried from the room.

Eleni didn't realize she was trembling until Gisele was gone. Immediately, she walked over to the bedroom door and locked it. She wasn't sure how much good locking the door was going to do since Gisele probably had a key, but it made her feel better—slightly more secure. Still, she couldn't stop herself from going through her jewelry box to see if anything had been taken.

To her relief, everything appeared to be in order. Nevertheless, she didn't intend to leave her jewelry box lying around anymore. She replaced the hairpins and shut the blue velvet box, securing the gold latch. Glancing around, she noticed the bedside table had a drawer. Of course, a drawer didn't compare with a safe, but it was better than nothing—especially now that she knew she couldn't leave things lying around for the staff to find.

She tucked away her jewelry box then closed the drawer and glanced out the window. Night had fallen. The sky was an inky, purple black with a crimson rim along the far horizon—still early. If Julian wasn't already up and about, he would be soon.

She cursed under her breath. She still needed to shower and get dressed before she went downstairs. The incident with Gisele had put her completely on guard, but it didn't change the fact that if she was going to catch Julian at breakfast, she'd have to hurry.

Julian stirred from a dream and stretched. With his eyes still closed, he rolled over and reached for Eleni, but his hand found only cool, satin sheets. His eyes popped open and dark brows pulled into a frown. He sat up on his elbow and raked his hand through his hair. The door was closed, and the room silent. When had she left his bed?

Their shared night of pleasure was seared on his memory. The scent of her blood beating with lust had nearly driven him mad with desire. He had not felt so alive in centuries before claiming her.

A twinge of disappointment plucked at him that she hadn't stayed until the lure of nightfall woke him. Exhaling deeply, he rolled onto his back and folded his arms behind his head. It had been a very long time since a woman had shared a bed with him. Sometimes, he called on Marguerite to sample a woman from her harem, but it was not the same as having an Acolyte of his own to share his bed. The women were faceless, nameless. Gone the next morning as their vampire mistress demanded of them, which suited him fine. Eleni was different, special in some way he couldn't put his finger on. And it wasn't simply because she answered to no one but him.

He tossed back the covers and sat on the edge of the bed, at once noticing the belt to his robe tossed across the chair. A flare of pride rose up in him. How deliciously willing she'd been. And she had not once asked him about his scars.

Remembering that he'd tossed his robe into the corner, Julian got up and walked around the bed to retrieve it since he still needed to shower and shave. On his way there, he stopped to pick up the heap of blankets that had fallen onto the floor at the foot of the bed. It was then he realized one of his sheets was missing. A sensual thrill skittered through him at the idea of Eleni walking through the house wrapped in a black silk sheet with nothing underneath.

A minute later, he found his robe discarded in the corner. He shook it out then slipped it on quickly, eager to seek out Eleni. She'd been abused, misled by her former Biter, so it didn't exactly come as a surprise that she'd left his room before his awakening, not with her trust issues. Nevertheless, he was eager for her company. If that meant he had to go to her, so be it.

On his way out the door, Julian was already thinking of all the wicked things he wanted to do to her. Like bend her over the desk in his office and kiss his way up those long legs. A slow smile twisted his lips.

He made his way over to the premiere suite and rapped his knuckles against the door. He didn't want to barge in on her, but when she didn't answer, he tried the door handle. The room was locked.

For a moment he stood staring at the door, his surprise slowly giving way to simmering anger. He turned away and started back down the hall to his own suite. If there was one thing he didn't approve of, it was being locked out of a room in his own house. Secrets had nearly killed him once, and he'd vowed long ago that would never happen again.

Eleni stepped out of the bathtub onto the mat and pulled a towel down off the wooden rack. Even after a long soak, she still felt jittery from her confrontation with Gisele, and now she had to get dressed and go downstairs to face Julian.

She couldn't make up her mind whether to tell him about Gisele trying on her clothes or not. Maybe if she hadn't already asked about his relationship with the woman, she wouldn't feel so weird about it. The last thing she wanted was for him to think she was jealous of the girl, or that she was out to get her fired, but at the same time, Eleni had the sneaking suspicion if she didn't handle the situation in the right way, Gisele would make misery for her later on.

Dread settled in her heart at the thought of having to watch her back all the time. It was too soon. She didn't want to go through that again. Was she even strong enough? She'd already fought that battle with Sabilla and Rubio, and it had nearly cost her both her health and her sanity.

When she'd left San Francisco, she'd thought, aside from the times she'd have to report to a probation officer from the council, that she was leaving that old life behind. After all, that had been the goal—to start a new life without the constant stress her former relationship had placed on her. And yet, even as she stood buffing herself dry with a bath towel, that familiar feeling of sadness and anxiety curled through her at the mere thought of the having to live that way again.

Eleni patted her face dry then wrapped her body in the towel before heading off to her closet to pick out something suitable to wear. If she could've come up with a passable excuse to hide away in her room all night, she would have done so.

Although she had managed to overcome her Biter's Addiction to the point that the urge to be bitten no longer ruled her life, she knew she was not the same woman as before. She couldn't handle stress very well. Confrontations got under her skin easily, and she didn't want Julian to see her shaken, especially after their first night together. He could get the wrong idea, and she didn't want him to think his bite had affected her negatively, when in truth, making love with him was probably the first time in months she had felt both sexy and at ease—a woman capable of continuing her life as an Acolyte.

After spending twenty minutes of fidgeting in front of the dresser mirror, Eleni finally admitted she was only putting off the inevitable. Dressed in a white sheath dress and strappy heels, she checked her nude lipstick before heading downstairs to find Julian.

At the base of the stairs, she veered right and walked through the open archway into the dining room. She shuffled to a stop just inside the room, her heart pitter-pattering at the sight of Julian sitting at the far end of the table, deep in conversation on his cell phone.

There was a magnetic quality about him she couldn't easily define. Her eyes drank in the sight of him. He'd showered and shaved, and wore his long hair pulled back in a sleek ponytail. Dressed in a crisp black suit jacket and a black silk shirt, he looked the epitome of male arrogance and beauty. It excited her, but at the same time, made her extremely nervous.

The chandelier was aglow over the formal table, which had been set for two, with a space for her at his right hand side. It came as a great relief that Gisele would not be joining them, not that she had expected it, but she had wondered if the woman might appear, perhaps to see if she mentioned anything about the incident upstairs. Thankfully, Julian sat alone. It would be much easier for her to talk to him about Gisele without an audience, although in her experience, being alone didn't necessarily mean they wouldn't somehow be overheard.

Almost as though Eleni's brooding thoughts had summoned her, Claudette bustled into the room pushing a serving cart. Her iron gray hair caught in a kerchief, she lifted the tray from the cart and set it on the table. She took one look at Eleni and nodded curtly. *"Bonsoir, Mademoiselle."*

Smartphone pressed to his ear, Julian looked up at her as she neared and did a double take. His eyes glittered with heat, but almost as soon as her gaze connected with his, his expression frosted over. He spoke quickly and quietly into his phone, and then hung up. Confused and wary, Eleni forced a smile as she approached Claudette and reached for a chair. "The coffee smells fantastic."

The housekeeper responded with a pleased grunt as she poured steaming coffee into the cups set out on the table. Eleni was just about to reach for her chair when Julian stood and came around the corner of the table to hold out the chair for her.

"Thank you," she murmured as she slipped into the seat, and allowed him to help her scoot toward the table. Something was up, she sensed it. The minute Julian took his seat again, his phone began to ring. Cursing under his breath, he picked it up long enough to silence it then set it down again.

Claudette uncovered a tray of fresh baked croissants, and the smell of warm bread made Eleni's stomach growl.

She hadn't had much to eat since her arrival in Ville Clemence, but the way Julian watched her with such focused intensity, she didn't know if she'd be able to eat anything.

By the time Claudette had left the room and closed the door to the kitchen entrance to allow them their privacy, her heart was hammering. Eleni stirred a spoonful of sugar into her coffee and when Julian still did not speak, she sighed. "Last night was wonderful, Julian. At least, it was for me." She looked up at him and studied his stern face. "If something is bothering you, I wish you would just tell me."

A storm brewed in his gray eyes. He rested his elbow on the table, and the way he traced the pad of his thumb over his lower lip made Eleni put down her spoon. A sinking feeling took root low in her belly when he ran his tongue over his fangs.

"The matter is simple—you are here for my pleasure. In return, I offer you the comfort and richness of my house. It is the old way, and I'm an unashamed traditionalist."

She frowned in confusion. "I'm grateful for everything you've done for me. I can't imagine what I've done to make you think otherwise."

"I don't like secrets." His voice was rough with anger. "There isn't a single room in this house I shouldn't have access to. That includes your suite. The doors in my house are to remain unlocked at all times. Do you understand?"

A chill prickled over her skin even as heat rushed into her face. "It wasn't my intention to lock you out. Gisele —"

"Do you understand?" He punctuated each word with cool authority.

"Perfectly," she said, and was about to excuse herself from the table when Julian threw another surprise her direction.

"I also will not tolerate mistreatment of my staff. Gisele told me you banned her from your room."

"Did she?" Her brows went up. "I suppose she also told you I found her playing dress up in my clothes? She was wearing my great-grandmother's hairpins."

If the news surprised him, his expression didn't show it.

"I'll investigate the matter, and if what you say is true, I'll speak to her about it."

"You do that," she said in a brittle voice. More than likely, Gisele had already fed him some reason for the locked door. How clever of her. From now on, she'd know to watch her back. "In the meantime, I'll take care of my own suite."

"As you choose," he grated, and picked up the silver blood cup from the table and sipped. "From now on, if you have a problem with one of my servants, you bring that issue to me and I will handle it."

Eleni lost all appetite for her breakfast. Julian's droll arrogance was too much for her. If not for her probation, she would've had a few choice words to say to her new Biter.

But really, what was the point of furthering the argument? The early evening was already ruined. He said he'd talk to Gisele, whatever that was worth.

She pretended an interest in the croissant on her plate, but the first bite she took was like ashes in her mouth. She picked at her food because Julian watched her, but the moment his cell phone rang, she saw her doorway to freedom. The second he picked up his phone and answered it, Eleni daubed at her mouth with the edge of the napkin and stood up from the table. She didn't wait to be excused, or bother to push her chair in. Why bother with niceties when he was already angry with her? She just wanted to be away from him, the sooner the better.

Hurt, angry, and confused, she took her coffee with her and headed toward the doorway, aware that he watched her back as she strode out of the dining room. Let him look. Clearly, the loyalty lines had been drawn well before her arrival. What a fool she'd been to think a day in bed with him would have made any impression on him. But then maybe that was where she kept failing—by mistakenly thinking she could be something more to a vampire than a blood meal and a body to warm someone's bed. The worst part of it was that she'd actually opened herself to the idea of being close to Julian—another failure on her part. One would think she'd have learned her lesson by now.

If holding her at a distance was how Julian wished to pursue their relationship, she could go along with that. In fact, she should count it as a blessing. She was far less likely to get her heart broken if she gave up any idea of being loved, and simply took her duty at face value.

Despite feeling like a grand fool, she squared her chin and started up the stairs to her room to setup her laptop and check her email. From now on, she'd make an effort to keep it light and impersonal with Julian. But even as she made that resolution, she wondered how she'd deal with Gisele if she ever found the woman in her room again.

Chapter Seven

Julian strode into his office and slammed the door behind him. He headed straight to the bar across the room and took a bottle of the Sévigné special *sang vin* from the refrigerated wine cabinet. His lips compressed into a grim line as he took out a glass and a corkscrew and set about opening the bottle. He much preferred to drink hot, rich blood straight from the source, but as always, he would do as he must.

The early evening was a total bust. If things had gone differently, he could have had his breakfast in bed—*Eleni*.

He'd waken up wanting her. It annoyed him to no end, but it wasn't so surprising, really. She was beautiful and willing, her skin as smooth and sweet as fresh cream. When he'd bitten her, her delicious blood had flowed into him like a potent liqueur. Just thinking about it made his heart pound and his body restless. He cursed himself for wanting her so strongly. Despite his anger, he craved her nearness, her touch. If she hadn't locked him out of her room, he would have instigated a repeat of the previous night. Instead, he'd chased her from the room like a shameless boar.

Frustrated, he poured a splash of blood wine into his glass then restoppered the bottle. Lifting the glass, he drank deeply, feeling the flare of heat from the wine and the blood restoring him. Out of breath, he lowered the cup and a gasp tore from his lungs. His heart thundering, he set the cup down and looked across the room at his desk.

Now he had Gisele to contend with. Already, it was beginning—the catty bickering among the women in his house. It was the very reason he had told Dominic he was not interested in reinstating a harem even to keep one Acolyte, although he had to admit now that Eleni was here, he couldn't imagine sending her away.

He turned on his computer and when the welcome screen came up, he typed in his password. If Gisele was in the house, he couldn't find her. Claudette had not seen her since the early evening, and he was willing to bet that was around the time she'd come into the dining room to tell him Eleni had banned her from her room. Frustrated also, because he'd wanted to make love to Eleni once more before the night began.

He picked up the phone on his desk and pressed the speed dial for the kitchen. The line rang in his ear, and he watched Claudette glance at the ringing phone. She stood the iron on its end, leaving it on the ironing board as she crossed the room and picked up the line.

"*Monsieur?*" she answered.

"Claudette, you are busy, so I won't keep you long. Did you send Gisele on an errand?"

"*Non, Monsieur.* I haven't seen nor spoken to her yet tonight."

"I see," he said, his mouth drawing into a thin line. "Thank you. I will let you get back to your doings."

He hung up the phone, and sat for a moment staring at the live feed. There could be no doubt. Gisele was not in the house. On a whim, he backtracked the video feed in the foyer, looking for her, and came across the moment he had walked downstairs an hour or so before.

Walking in and out of view of the camera, Gisele paced in the east hallway, outside the small parlor, and it appeared as though she was talking on her cell phone. When he came into view on the stairs, Gisele stopped pacing, pulled her hand down from her face and tucked something into her pocket—the phone. She came into the foyer, and he remembered that she had called out to him then.

There was no sound while skipping through the frames, but it didn't matter, he vividly recalled the conversation. How furious she'd been! On the computer screen, he watched her storm across the room, her hands clenched into fists as she met him at the bottom of the stairs. Right away, judging by the proud jut of her chin and the gleam in her dark eyes, he had sensed that something was up. Out of breath, her face red, she dove right into an angry rant about Eleni. She'd spoken so fast her words ran together, a scathing five minute spew session about why he should never have allowed her in the house.

Of course, Gisele hadn't told him why Eleni had banned her from the premiere suite, but he'd suspected a disagreement of some kind. He couldn't guess what it had been about, but Eleni was…secretive. He could not think of a better term for it, and Gisele could be pushy. He should have corrected her behavior long ago, but she knew her limits with him, and he had not seen the need. Not with only himself, Claudette, and Henri in the house.

"Let us see where you have gone, hmm?" he muttered to Gisele's image on the screen as he fast forwarded through the footage.

Julian frowned as he continued to scan through the frames. When he left the room, she stared after him, chewing her nails. It seemed as though she didn't know quite what to do. She glanced up the stairs, then toward the hallway leading back to his office. Wrapping her arms around herself, she walked over to the front door and paced.

For several frames, she lingered in the entryway, then out of nowhere, two beams of light passed over the stained glass insets along either side of the front door—headlights from a car pulling up the driveway.

Julian's eyes narrowed. He hadn't realized anyone had stopped by.

As Gisele's image climbed into the black car, he froze the recording, and with the touch of a few keys, he switched to the driveway camera and resumed watching the video from a new angle, rubbing his chin as he studied the luxury car.

The driver was indeterminable. It could have been anyone. It could have been one of her friends from the village, although he didn't think so. A vampire possibly, since the windows were tinted, but if it was, he couldn't imagine who it could be. He had introduced her to no one but Marguerite, and given their history together, it seemed highly unlikely she would go there.

He tried to zoom in on the license plate, but the grainy resolution made the numbers and letters blow apart into anonymous gray pixels.

Frowning, Julian let out a deep breath and closed the replay window, bringing up the main security screen. He was usually so involved with the running of the vineyard he rarely paid attention to Gisele—where she went and who she spent time with. From now on, he would have to keep closer tabs on her.

It was on his mind to go back through the footage to see the argument between Gisele and Eleni firsthand, but no…for now, that was finished. As vital as it was to know what was going on in his household at all times, it wasn't his intention to betray the trust or privacy of anyone living with him. No, the recordings would be there later, should he choose to go over them.

He moved the mouse, dragging his cursor across the screen to click the icon he needed to turn off the display, but at the last second he hesitated. After the poor start to the evening, he couldn't help himself. Instead of shutting down, he brought up the room by room display to look for Eleni. It was almost a compulsion, if for no other reason but to look at her face.

Julian frowned. For years, Marguerite had been telling him it had been too long since he had a woman of his own, and he was beginning to believe she was right. Eleni might have been in his house for less than two days, but already he couldn't keep his mind off her.

Chapter Eight

"I suppose you plan to hide yourself away in here all night?"

Eleni looked up from her laptop and found Julian standing there, watching her from the opposite side of the small patio table. Still peevish with him for their earlier argument, she sat straighter and pushed her dark-rimmed glasses up the bridge of her nose. "The thought had occurred to me, yes."

The central fountain gurgled continually, the white noise soothing. In fact, Eleni found everything about this room comforting—the flagstone floors and bamboo rushes, the maze of hot house jungle plants. It gave her the illusion of being hidden and safe. If she could not have privacy in her own suite, she could have it here without worry. She'd been sitting in here for hours, working on a digital art project for her online gallery, and until Julian came along, not one person had come into the room to disturb her.

He strode forward and held out a glass of wine for her. "You weren't at dinner." The sleeves of his black shirt were rolled up, revealing muscular arms with many glossy scars. They did nothing to distract from his handsomeness, but she did not take the drink.

She turned her attention back to her laptop. "I had Claudette bring a tray to me in here."

"Convenient, I suppose," he said as he set the wine down on the table next to her laptop. "But a lonely choice for us both."

"Lonely is better than being fussed at," Eleni said, and turned her attention back to her computer.

"Ah. You are still angry with me." The amusement in his voice set her off.

"And I shouldn't be?" she asked in a chilly voice. She knew he baited her, but she couldn't help herself. He had her attention now. She took off her glasses and set them on the table then looked up at him.

"You've told me frankly about the rules of the house," she said, forcing herself to keep her tone level. "I can accept that. Whatever you want to think about me, I'm not a troublemaker. I'm not here because I disrespected my former Biter. I was good to Rubio, and I was loyal to him, even when I knew he wasn't loyal to me. Still, I did whatever he asked of me, even to the detriment of my own health. If that makes me a disgrace, then what can I say?" She shrugged, then abruptly reached out and shut the lid of her laptop.

"The thing is," she continued, "when Dominic told me he was sending me to France to get the council off my back, I didn't expect you to love me. I didn't even expect you to be loyal to me. I still don't. I'm not the young fool I once was. If anything, I'd want you to be honest with me, and that's what I'm putting to you now. I want to hear it from you directly, Julian. What is your relationship with Gisele? Is she your lover? Because I get the feeling she's used to special treatment." She sat back and searched his guarded expression. "Whatever you tell me, I will believe you, and I won't bring it up to you again. But, as your protégé—your première, if that is what I truly am to you, then I deserve to know. And I'd rather hear the explanation from you than from her."

The question seemed to take him aback. Once he had a moment to let her words sink in, he blew out a breath and smoothed a hand over his hair. Eleni crossed her arms and waited while he pulled out one of the chairs so he could sit down.

"Gisele is not, and has never been, my lover. Rest assured, that is true." He sighed. "Perhaps she does receive special treatment. For that, I am to blame. She grew up here, in this house, after all."

"She was a born here?"

"Oh, no, no…" Frowning, he shook his head. "She was born in the village, although she might as well have been born here. Her mother had worked in my household as a trusted servant for probably fifteen years. Gisele's mother was named Aline-Marie, and she came to work for me when she herself was fairly young."

"Where is she now—the mother?"

"She's buried outside of Ville Cleménce in the cemetery of a little church. I was sad to hear that she had died. Aline-Marie was a trusted servant, you understand? Her familial line went back some hundred and fifty years. She was a good girl. Reliable." A slight frown troubled his features, and his eyes took on a faraway look. "I have never forbidden my staff from taking lovers, and I knew Aline-Marie began seeing a carpenter, a man in the village named Hugo Gespar, not long after she took up residence with me. He was a good deal older than her, but that did not stop her from falling madly in love with him. One night in late spring, she came to my office and told me she intended to leave her position in my home, because she wished to marry her lover—this Hugo. I granted her that right, and at her request, I planned to write to the council to remove her name from servitude."

Eleni gaped at him. "She actually asked you to do that? To sever her familial line?" She'd never heard of a servant requesting such a thing. It took generations of loyal service to a vampire household for a bloodline to be considered worthy of such an honor.

"What could I do? Change her mind? She loved him. Nothing else mattered to her but Hugo." Julian shrugged. "She told me she never intended to return to a servant's life, so why would she need to remain under the umbrella of security my household provided, especially when Hugo was there to provide for her? Too, I think she didn't want her children to be labeled as servants. In the end, who knows what she was thinking? I never asked her." He looked away toward the glass wall and beyond it, to the black, lightless infinity behind the house. "I fully intended to see to her wishes, but it was a hard year for the vineyard. I was busy with so many things and never got around to writing to the council in Paris to have her branch of the familial line stricken from the book of names."

Frowning, Eleni reached for the glass of wine. "What happened then?"

"I lost track of Aline-Marie once she moved out. A few years later," he said, his mouth drew down as he thought back, "perhaps it was a year and a half? Two years? Hugo came here and dropped off Gisele at my doorstep. She was just a baby, less than a year old. Hugo didn't speak to me, of course, but he told Claudette that Aline-Marie had died in an accident, and that he couldn't take care of the girl."

Eleni shook her head. "Why did he bring her here and not to an orphanage?"

He shrugged. "Perhaps he assumed we knew her family. I don't really know. As I said, I didn't speak to him. It was Claudette who took the girl in. I didn't approve at first, and I'm ashamed to say I even resented her being here. It seemed wrong to be raising another man's child, but then it was also Aline-Marie's child, so I allowed it. About six months later, a story cropped up in the newspaper about Hugo. The police had arrested him outside of Paris. It was reported that Aline-Marie had been killed in a car accident, but there were questions surrounding her death. Hugo was tried and convicted of killing his wife, whom he believed was having an affair. I think maybe he doubted Gisele was his child, but there is no mistake in my mind. Aline-Marie loved him too much to hurt him in that way."

Eleni shuddered. "That's awful."

"Indeed," Julian agreed with her. "The police came here later. They planned to take Gisele away. Claudette had grown attached to her by then. She was beside herself with grief. It made me look at Gisele in a new way. I felt sorry for her. She had no family, but came from a long line of trusted servants. Since I had not yet written to the council to remove her mother from servitude, I decided to leave her status intact. I figured Aline-Marie's heritable title would at least give the child a life, a place to belong."

"So, you raised her, then?" Eleni could see why Gisele might look at the chateau as her home, rather than being a live-in member of Julian's serving staff.

Eyes dark with caution, he laughed. The low, throaty sound told her he had no desire to make such a claim. "I took very little part in her upbringing. I gave her shelter and paid her expenses, but I know nothing about children. When Gisele was a year old, I sent her to live with Marguerite. That way, Claudette could keep her position and still visit the child. I thought it best to see her brought up among women, at least until she was of proper age to take her mother's place in my household. And the women in her harem doted over her. She was a beautiful child, very bright. When she grew up, I sent her to boarding school, and then on to university. She came here during the holidays to be groomed for service. But that hardly matters. As you see, you have nothing to worry about when it comes to Gisele. I watched her grow up. I would not say she is so much like a daughter, but I compare her to a beloved niece."

Eleni swallowed hard. She knew what it felt like to lose her mother, and to have her home disrupted. If not for her older sister, Anya, she would have been entirely alone. When Anya had taken her bows as a debutante into vampire society, Eleni had resented it—the suitors, her sister, the entire process. She had perceived it as a threat to their small family. She had nightmares that a vampire would fall in love with her sister, sponsor her, and take her away.

It was possible that Gisele looked at her as a similar threat. After all, she had joined the household rather suddenly. While that still did not excuse her for the invasion of her privacy, she couldn't help but soften toward her a little.

"Give it time. The two of you will become accustomed to each other." The way he said it told her that he expected nothing less. He stood up then and walked around to her side of the table. "If you're finished with whatever you're doing, let's go sit in front of the fire— maybe, watch TV?" His hand slid along her inner elbow, a gentle caress. "It's been a tough start to the day, and I'm lonely for the company of my new protégé."

Eleni hesitated. She knew it wasn't smart to cave so easily, but how could she refuse when his voice softened in that way? All it took was one glance into his guarded eyes, and she sensed something vulnerable there, a hidden need for affection that he would never openly admit.

Eleni sighed and got up from the table. "Fine, just give me ten minutes to take my computer up to my room, and I'll rejoin you downstairs."

Julian picked up her hand and kissed it. "I'll be waiting."

Chapter Nine

"Marguerite, come in." Eleni held the front door open for the vampiress while she entered the house. In those few moments, the frigid wind had swirled a good amount of snow onto the entryway rug, where it quickly melted. The vampiress stood at the edge of the rug and began shrugging out of her red woolen coat. "Whatever made you want to stand out front? Why didn't you come in through the garage?"

"I thought about it, but I didn't want to disturb anyone. There was the possibility I'd catch you while you were entertaining Julian," the vampiress said as she handed her coat to Eleni, who dusted the melting snowflakes from the shoulders before hanging it in the entryway closet. "I figured if no one answered the door, you were indisposed."

"No, not this early in the evening," she said as she closed the closet door. "I was in the sunroom, writing an email to my sister—nothing that couldn't wait."

"Then I'm glad I decided to go ahead and visit." Marguerite smoothed her hands along the sleeves of her silver, satin shirt. "I hope you don't mind me dropping by like this. It's been a month since your arrival, and I was curious to see how you're adjusting."

"You're always welcome here, Marguerite. I'm sure you know that." It was the truth. Julian would never turn away his cousin.

Over the past few weeks, Eleni had come to realize how much Julian cared about the people around him—Marguerite, Claudette, and Henri. Gisele was still a sticky spot with her, but so far they had managed to avoid each other, and Eleni had decided early on she could live with that if they could keep their distance.

Melted snowflakes glistened in Marguerite's auburn hair as Eleni guided her into the small parlor, which was lit with a small crystal chandelier that threw a soft light around the room that was both pleasing and easy on a vampire's eyes. Eleni didn't often come in here, but the room was warm and comfortable, with heavy black leather furniture and a large fireplace.

Marguerite needed no one to guide her—she walked right over to one of the couches and sat down heavily, blowing out a breath. She stretched her arms along the back of the couch, her crimson smile at once both devious and beguiling. "So, tell me how you're doing? It has been so boring at home, and I am curious. I want to know everything. Your hearing is only a few months away? Are you looking forward to it?"

Eleni gave her a wide-eyed look that made the sophisticated vampiress laugh. "I suppose not. But you seem to be adjusting. Surely, that will be considered in your favor?"

"I hope so," Eleni told her warily as she sank down into one of the chairs opposite Marguerite. "I know my way around the house now, and I feel comfortable with Claudette and Henri. I'm trying my best to fit in."

"And you are doing a fine job of it," the vampiress said softly. "Yes, I believe you'll do fine. I will put in a recommendation for you. You're a scrupulous girl. By the way, Julian is here, yes?"

"He should be in his office still. I visited him earlier tonight—I stayed until he got very busy then thought I'd leave him to his work. You want me to call him for you?"

"Julian and his work…" Marguerite made a moue of disapproval. "I had hoped you'd break him of that habit. Ah, but never mind, I didn't come over to see him." Her eyes brightened. "He will be curious that I have befriended you, but I have heard of your line before, you know?"

That surprised her. "You have?"

"Oh, indeed. Julian spoke highly of your sister, Anya. He told me that our cousin Dominic entered into the blood bond with her. That is no small event. All the relatives were informed of the match. A new vampiress is something to celebrate. The Sévigné branch has not had a new vampiress since I was turned…and that has been some time ago."

"I had no idea." Eleni swallowed hard. She didn't mention that she'd been too sick at the time to realize the significance of what went on around her. The uncomfortable realization that she had likely missed many important things that year made her squirm in her seat.

On top of that, she found it hard to imagine a celebration around her sister's transformation. Anya had been dying when Dominic made the snap decision to turn her. Eleni wondered if Marguerite knew. The transformation had been under very unusual circumstances. As romantic as it was, Eleni didn't anticipate any man would do something so honorable for her.

Not knowing what else to say, she forced a smile. "Dominic and Anya seem happy together. From what I could tell, they are nearly inseparable—very much in love. We should all be so lucky."

"True…true…" Her voice drifted away, her eyes for a moment distant and dreamy. A smile pulled her back to the here and now. "So, tell me, how do you like the chateau? What have you been doing to pass the time?"

"Marguerite," Julian's throaty voice chided her from the doorway. Eleni turned in the chair, glancing back to see him with his hand braced high on the jamb. "You sound like you're giving an interview. You plan to steal my protégé?"

"Julian." Marguerite beamed. She rose from her chair as he came into the room. She met him halfway and greeted him with an air-kiss by both cheeks, then she took his hand and drew him into the seating area. At last, she let him go and sat down again, gesturing him toward one of the remaining chairs.

"Of course, he would see an ulterior motive in all this…" Marguerite gave Eleni a flabbergasted look before turning her attention to Julian. "I've missed you, silly man. You're always hiding away in this old house."

"I have no reason to hide," he said as he flopped down in the chair closest to the fire. He looked at Eleni, and a small thrill passed over her, making her shiver. He looked as though he wanted to lay her out across the couch and eat her alive.

"Gisele," Marguerite called out suddenly.

Eleni jumped at the sudden change in the vampiress's voice. It shifted from friendly to authoritative without a shred of warning. A sudden tension filled the room and Eleni's heart began to race. She hadn't been aware of Gisele's nearness, but apparently she had been close enough to hear their conversation.

A feeling of unease slithered through her. She'd been too focused on Julian to notice where Gisele had come from. It appeared she had been passing by in the hallway when Marguerite spotted her, perhaps coming from her bedroom, which was located downstairs, at the far end of the east wing.

Gisele looked anything but happy when she came to the doorway. Her brown eyes were narrowed, her chin lifted to a haughty degree. "You called, Madame?"

Marguerite's face had become a mask of seriousness, yet her state of repose hadn't changed. Her right arm was propped against the pillows, and the other arm was stretched out along the tops of the cushions. But there was no mistaking her change in mood. Her eyes had darkened to the color of onyx. Glossy and fierce, they gleamed like a viper's. Indeed, she looked like a serpent waiting for the right moment to strike.

She smiled cordially. "Be a good girl. Fetch a tray of wine from the kitchens for us, *s'il vous plaît.*"

Despite her civil tone, Eleni could clearly see she'd just delivered an order, not a request.

A strange look came over Gisele's face, a cross between embarrassment and thinly veiled hate. Rosy color swept into her cheeks in high, bright spots. Her dark eyes flicked briefly toward Eleni before she bowed out of the room with a curt, "Of course."

Silence hung heavy in the room once she had gone. Marguerite crossed her long legs and tossed back her hair. A smug smile stretched her lips.

"Gita, you really shouldn't goad her like that." Julian's voice rumbled with disapproval.

"I do not goad her." Marguerite shot a cool glance his direction, clearly challenging him. "Gisele is a servant, so I asked her to serve."

Eleni didn't say a word. Clearly, this was an old argument, and she had no desire to get involved.

Marguerite gradually steered the conversation back on track, but the easy camaraderie they'd shared before

Gisele's arrival had been lost. Eleni was glad Julian took up the conversation with his cousin. The brief incident had made Eleni anxious and uncomfortable. She found herself counting the minutes until she could escape to her room, but Marguerite seemed adamant on staying, at least until Gisele returned. Eleni didn't think it had the first thing to do with the vampiress wanting a drink. The way Marguerite watched the door reminded her of a hungry cat preparing to pounce on a helpless morsel.

In the end, Gisele denied her the satisfaction of a second attack. Claudette brought in the tray of the wine.

Julian said nothing. He seemed to barely notice, but it clearly didn't escape Marguerite's attention that Gisele had not returned. Her brows lifted when the elderly woman offered Julian the first glass of wine from the tray, then Marguerite. Marguerite took Eleni's glass from the tray as well and served Eleni by her own hand.

"*À votre santé*," Marguerite said, raising her glass in a toast to Eleni, who lifted her glass as well.

"*Santé.*"

Julian lifted his glass, but said nothing. He sipped his wine in silence, his eagle eyes sending an uneasy chill through Eleni from across the room.

They spent half the night listening to Marguerite recall amusing family stories. She did most of the talking until around 3:00 AM, when she looked at her diamond wristwatch and hissed. "Mon Dieu, look at the time," she tittered. "It will be dawn before you know it. Dauphine will be upset with me, for sure."

She got up and stretched her long legs, and Eleni rose with her.

"I'll get your coat for you," she offered.

"Wait, *chére.*" She turned to Julian, who still lounged rakishly in the high-backed chair. Marguerite leaned down and gave him a peck on the cheek. "You have a most charming protégé."

"Agreed…" he said in that dark, cryptic tone that made a chill run down Eleni's spine.

Marguerite sighed. "I'm sorry I must go. I do miss talking to you like this, cousin, but I'm afraid if I'm not home soon, my harem will think I have left them."

"Do your ladies truly believe you would leave them so willingly?" he teased.

She cackled merrily. "No, but my premiere, she may think I have left for Paris without her. She is continually begging to go. I tell her I will consider it; that I will ask to use your townhouse for a vacation. And I do consider it…briefly." Her eyes twinkled with mischief. "You know as well as I do, there is nothing in the city for me."

"A new protégé or two, perhaps?"

"You speak as if I don't already have enough household drama." Marguerite tsked and shook her head. "Come, Eleni, walk me out. You will allow her, won't you, Julian?"

He shrugged, eyes glittering. "But of course."

The way he sloshed his wine in his glass told Eleni there was more on his mind than what he was saying, but she didn't have time to try and decipher his body language. Marguerite had started toward the door, so Eleni followed her around the corner into the entryway. It was her duty to entertain guests, and take care of even the smallest courtesies, but when she went to retrieve Marguerite's coat, the vampiress shooed her away.

"No need to fuss. I can manage a closet door by myself," she chided softly.

She waited while Marguerite pulled on her red coat, and fished in her pocket for the keys. A feeling of nervous anxiety crawled through her at the serious expression on the other woman's face, when at last Marguerite turned to her and said, "Shall we go?"

"One minute," Eleni said, and pulled a tan jacket down for herself before following the woman outside to a sleek, red sports car.

She sensed the vampiress wanted to tell her something important, but was wary of doing so within Julian's house. Anxious to hear what Marguerite had to say, she stepped out into the portico and slipped her arms into the jacket as the cold slammed into her, and her first night's breath frosted on the air.

The sky was a cloudy, starless black, so dark that the outside light near the front door gleamed gold, like a tiny captured fire within the brass sconce. The soles of her leather riding boots crunched over the gravel.

How Marguerite managed to cross the driveway in heels without stumbling, Eleni could only guess. As the vampiress reached for the door of her car, she stopped short and turned her head to look up at the house. A feeling of chill warning flowed through Eleni when she realized Marguerite was looking directly at her bedroom window.

"You see that room there?" The vampiress nodded toward the premiere suite. "The fire that burned Julian started there. It had to be two hundred years ago if it were a day."

Eleni found herself holding her breath.

Marguerite sighed. Her eyes reflected the dim light, shifting from dark to bright green as she turned her head to look at Eleni. "That was another lifetime, it seems. Julian had a harem then—roughly twelve young women much like yourself, although I dare say none were as personable or as lovely. Julian left them to their jealousies, and in my opinion, I believe he thought it to be rather amusing that they fought over him so. He took more than a fair amount of time in choosing a favorite, but even then he refused to declare a woman his premiere protégé. In the end, it was their squabbling over who would be his premiere that ultimately led to the fire that burned him."

Eleni was stunned. She shook her head. "I had no idea."

Shrewd eyes regarded her. "I am not surprised. Julian…he doesn't like to talk about the past. He was burnt beyond recognition, and it was thought for a time he would not live. We were all very worried for him, not only because we love him so, but because he was an Elder even then, and the last male in our familial bloodline carrying the Sévigné name. The news was the talk of society for many years. Even after all this time, every once in a while, rumors crop up that Julian is dead."

"That's awful," Eleni whispered.

"And sadly, that is not all of it." Marguerite went on. "It took a great many vampires, including your brother-in-law, to come to his care. It takes a lot of blood, powerful blood, to heal that kind of damage. The Russian side of the family was called in to help with his healing. I was very young then, but I remember it vividly. There were those who felt he should be allowed to die. Dominic fought adamantly against it. It was a horrible tragedy…and Julian was not the only victim. The girl he favored at the time, Chloe, a young protégé who I believe he was considering for his première, died in the blaze, along with six…perhaps seven, others of his household. Their families were most aggrieved, and Julian was made to pay recompense to each of them. That in itself was a great scandal. It also very nearly bankrupted him."

A cold feeling settled in the pit of her stomach as Marguerite looked up at the house again. Eleni had no idea why she was telling her any of this. To upset her? Perhaps even to frighten her? If so, her ploy was working.

"From the look of it now, you can hardly tell it ever burned. The newer stone is slightly a different shade, but then again, weathering could have done the same." She shrugged. "No one in the village remembers much, I think. Historians, perhaps, but who are they? I suppose the house knows. It's a shame jealousy led to so much destruction, no?"

Eleni shook her head. "I don't know what to say."

"There is nothing to say. It simply is, and I thought you needed to know. Now, I should be going." She reached out and squeezed Eleni's hand. "I hope you do not take any of this the wrong way. I do like you, Eleni. Very much. You remind me of myself when I was young and worried about my status in life. That's why I'm going to warn you to watch out for Gisele. She is an ambitious girl, and men, even my dear Julian, are not always capable of seeing the dark heart beneath a beautiful surface. I would be very sad to see history repeat itself."

Without another word, Marguerite got in her car, casting a brief smile at Eleni before she closed the door. Eleni stood frozen, staring as the vampiress cranked the car, turned on her lights, then pulled out of the driveway, the car tires crunching over the loose gravel. Eleni followed the red glow of the taillights until they disappeared from sight. Chilled by Marguerite's warning, she wrapped her arms around herself and walked back into the house.

Chapter Ten

Eleni locked the front door and hung up the coat she'd worn to walk Marguerite to her car. The house seemed quiet now, almost empty in her absence. One certainly couldn't say that Marguerite wasn't vivacious. Her personality could fill a room.

Even so, Eleni wished Marguerite hadn't told her about the origin of the fire—about the deaths. Aside from the fact that Julian had been badly burned, she hadn't known much more than what Dominic had told her, and he hadn't mentioned there had been so many victims. She had automatically assumed he had been alone in the house when the blaze started. Of course, thinking on it now, that didn't seem plausible. There would have been at least a dozen staff members to support such a large household, and then there were the Acolytes themselves.

She shivered at the thought of a fire spreading through the premiere suite. How many women had died there, trapped in that room? Eleni gave herself a mental shake.

The deaths of Julian's former protégés were too much to think about. What a terrible tragedy. She prayed silently they had not suffered. It frightened her to think of those poor women being engulfed in flames. No wonder Julian ruled his household as he did. Why he demanded there be no secrets, no locked doors. She understood and couldn't blame him now that she knew the truth.

She headed back toward the small parlor to meet up with Julian. Earlier, he had talked about spending the early morning hours together in his suite, on the rug in front of the fireplace, just the two of them. Desperate for a distraction, she sought him out, planning to take him up on his offer. If he would take her, she wanted to go right now.

Tracing her fingers along the polished woodwork as she walked down the hallway, she looked down at her shoes as she rounded the corner into the small parlor where she had last seen him.

"Julian, I—" Eleni froze in the doorway when she realized that he wasn't in the room. Bent over the coffee table, picking up everyone's wine glasses and putting them on the tray, Gisele looked up at the sound of her voice. At once, her expression grew cold. She stood straight, her eyes bright and angry.

"What do *you* want?"

Her tone gave Eleni pause. "Sorry, I thought Julian was still in here."

"If he was still here, do you think I'd be carrying dishes?" She tossed the rag down on the silver tray and turned to face Eleni then, her hands clenched into fists at her side. "You know something? You're just like her—Marguerite. So full of yourself. You both make me ill."

Eleni's brows shot up. She wasn't used to dealing with such open hostility. The women in her former harem had been very discreet, even more so with their gossip. Then again, she had to remind herself Gisele wasn't an Acolyte.

"I've done nothing to you," Eleni reminded her in a level tone. "If you have a problem with Marguerite, I suggest you take it up with her."

She turned to leave the room, but Gisele's loud scoff stopped her.

"You think I don't see right through you?" Gisele snapped. Eleni glanced back, and Gisele glared at her in disdain. "You think I can't tell that you don't want me here?" The beautiful face narrowed into a sly expression that dared Eleni to deny it. She couldn't. Although she had never put it to actual thought before this moment, life would be so much easier if Gisele was not in the house.

Eleni straightened. "You said it, I didn't."

"You didn't have to say it. It's obvious just by looking at you."

A smug smile crossed Gisele's face. Tossing her hair back, she took two steps forward, her hands clenched into fists at her sides. It didn't take much to see Gisele wanted to hit her. Eleni's heart rate kicked up a notch. She didn't know what the girl intended to do, but she braced herself for a possible fight.

"I suppose you found Marguerite's attack on me terribly amusing."

Attack on her? Eleni frowned. "I'm not Marguerite. Besides, Julian defended you."

"Of course he did," Gisele snapped at her. "How else would he react? Julian cares for me."

Eleni flinched at the unwelcome stab of jealousy that washed over her. "Is that so unusual? It seems to me Julian cares for everyone he considers his responsibility."

Gisele's breathing quickened, and her face became a mask of barely restrained fury. Her jaw clenched tight, and she took a step forward and jabbed a finger at Eleni. "You have no idea what I'm capable of," she growled under her breath. "Stay out of my way, you little bitch, or I will make you regret ever setting foot in this house."

She went back to the table and snatched up the tray with the wineglasses. If Eleni hadn't moved out of the way, Gisele would have bumped her with the tray when she stormed out of the room.

Alone in the silence of the room, Eleni took a deep breath and laid a hand against her forehead in an effort to calm her jangling nerves. She didn't know what she was going to do about Gisele. She didn't want to complain to Julian, but how would she ever find peace in his household if the girl insisted on warring with her again and again?

A deep frown etched Julian's brow as he paced in front of the fireplace in his office. It seemed childish to be so grossly annoyed at Marguerite, but he couldn't help himself. One glance at his cousin told him everything. There was no mistaking the attraction he saw in her eyes. So far, she had kept a friendly distance, but tonight he found himself on guard, analyzing her every word.

Never mind how many times had he entertained a woman from Marguerite's harem, Eleni was different. There was more to be had than the pleasure her body promised. She had a reserved yet vulnerable quality about her. It was almost as if she had judged the world and now held it at a distance, but at the same time, she was neither aloof nor cynical. Her complexity drew him to her more than she probably realized. It troubled him that Marguerite seemed attuned to it also.

He glanced at the large wall clock and decided they had been outside talking for close to fifteen minutes. Raking a hand through his hair, he paced. He made it a point not to run to the security feeds to check up on them. He relied on that too much already, and there was no excuse for it. At every turn, Eleni had proven sensitive to his needs, and he wanted to give her space. But, at the same time, he didn't like the idea of her being alone with Marguerite, which was funny because it had never bothered him with any of his Acolytes in the past. It shouldn't have mattered now, but he got the distinct impression that if he hadn't favored Eleni upon her arrival, Marguerite would have been more than willing to take her off his hands.

Tired of waiting, Julian left his office to tell her to come inside. If Marguerite wanted company, she could find it with her own protégés. He walked down the corridor, his eyes on the front door, but as he came into the entryway, he caught a glimpse of movement out of the corner of his eye. Eleni walked out of the small parlor. She had her arms wrapped around herself as if she were cold.

A fierce sense of protectiveness flared inside him. Thinking of nothing but her comfort, Julian started toward her, reaching her in three long strides.

"What's wrong? You look shaken."

Eleni jumped at the authoritative sound in Julian's voice. She'd been so lost in thought she hadn't realized he was near. It was a relief to see him striding toward her, and she had to stop herself from throwing her arms around his neck when he was at last close enough to touch.

He cupped the sides of her face and smoothed back her hair, his frown deepening. "It's something Marguerite said to you, isn't it?" His eyes were furious.

She shook her head gently. "No, it's nothing like that." She laid her hands over his and drew them down, kissing the back of first one hand then the other, a gesture of proof. "Really, I'm fine. A little tired, is all." That much was true.

"You're sure?" Concern glittered in his pale eyes. "It's not your Biter's Addiction, is it? We've been careless lately. I bit you just yesterday. Perhaps it is too much, too soon. Tell me what to do and—"

"No." Eleni shook her head, her face hot with embarrassment to hear him speak of her illness in such a way. It was the last thing she'd expected to hear from him. "It's not that. I promise, it isn't."

"Tell me, then. What's the matter?"

She let out a deep sigh, and confessed. "Gisele is upset. Marguerite rattled her, I think. I went into the parlor and she was very angry with me."

He frowned. "Not possible…" he said in a voice that was both rumbling and tense. He picked up her hand and took a step back, drawing her away from the wall with him. "Gisele can be defensive, but I assure you, she is not angry with you. I was there. You did nothing, and you should know Gisele and Marguerite have a longstanding feud between them. There's nothing either of us can do about it, so it's best to let it be."

She didn't doubt his claim that there was a feud between the two women, but Eleni knew for certain Gisele disliked her, if for no other reason than having caught her unawares that morning raiding her wardrobe. Even so, Eleni wasn't about to argue with him. He gave her a gentle tug, and she stood away from the wall.

"Where are we going?" she asked.

"To my office, where no one will disturb us. I have a fire going and a bottle of wine on ice. A brand new Sévigné white I am considering for distribution. I want you to share it with me."

Secretly relieved that her job as hostess was over for the evening, a glass of wine and Julian's full attention sounded heavenly. She took his hand without protest and allowed him to guide her through the house to his office.

Chapter Eleven

Two nights after Marguerite's unexpected visit, Julian wandered into the solarium where Eleni stretched out on her favorite wicker lounge chair surrounded by palm leaves and was flipping through a magazine. He had been quiet, almost reserved since Marguerite's visit, but Eleni didn't press him for a reason. If she had learned anything since joining his household, it was that Julian was a private person. She knew he wouldn't tell her what was on his mind unless he knew of a way to fix the problem immediately.

It was a little after ten o'clock, but he sat down with a heavy sigh in one of the chairs across from her.

"You look tired," she commented, eyeing him over the rim of her glasses.

"I feel tired."

Eleni chuckled.

"You don't feel sorry for me at all, do you?" He folded his arms behind his head and regarded her with an almost petulant expression.

Stifling a smile, she tapped her index finger against her tongue and turned yet another page. "Not the least little bit."

He scoffed. "You're shameless, *chére*. Absolutely heartless. Especially since it is your fault I've been getting so little sleep." He leaned forward, captured the edge of her magazine, and dragged it away.

"Now who's heartless?" Eleni teased. "I was reading that."

The devilish man tossed her magazine aside as if daring her to do something about it. Then he reached out and caught her hand, pulling her off the lounger. She crawled onto his lap, straddling him, and Julian locked his arms around her and gripped her bottom, urging her to grind against him. "I'm finished with my work for the night, so I was thinking maybe you'd want to go upstairs and get dressed."

"Don't you mean get undressed?" She kissed his forehead, then the side of his neck.

"Mm, I suppose you could do that. But I'm not so sure they would let you into Chez Gerard…although with your delicious body, I could be mistaken about that."

She pulled back and looked at him. "Chez Gerard? You're taking me to dinner?"

"I thought about it, yes." A wicked light came into his eyes. "Is that so strange?"

"You have to ask?" Eleni laughed softly. "You rarely go anywhere."

He shrugged. "Only because I am usually so busy—but not tonight. I've made an exception and cleared my schedule. It will do us both some good to have a break, don't you think? I know it will benefit me," he drawled. "I've thought of nothing but you since I awakened." He distracted himself with the gap of her shirt. She sighed in contentment when he unfastened one of her buttons and nuzzled her breasts, kissing them before scraping his fangs playfully against a tender curve.

After a moment, he growled low in his chest and swatted her on the bottom. "Unless you want to spend the evening in bed, you best stop teasing me." His words sent a small thrill through her.

"Oh, all right," she said on sigh. "If you insist." Eleni bit back a grin as she slithered off his lap, making it a point to rub herself against his erection.

Julian hissed. "Little devil, go get dressed." His eyes lingered on her breasts as she stood up and adjusted her shirt. "I'll call ahead and reserve a table."

"I'll meet you downstairs in fifteen minutes," Eleni said, and blew him a kiss on her way out the door.

Eleni stood in front of the dresser mirror to put on a pair of silver dangle earrings that matched the shimmery, form fitted dress that Anya had bought for her as a farewell gift just before she'd left for France. Wearing it made her feel closer to her sister, more confident. Perfect for times like this, when she wanted to make an impression, but worried her nervousness would get in the way of enjoying the evening out.

After coiling her hair into a loose chignon, she pinned it in place then sat on the edge of her bed and slipped on a matching pair of silvery high heels.

At the last minute, she remembered the chinchilla coat that Julian had placed in the closet for her as an arrival gift. Now would be a perfect time to wear it. However, when she stepped into the walk-in closet, the coat was not where she had left it—the very first garment on the left side rack. She tried to remember if she had moved it. After the night she'd caught Gisele trying on her clothes, she'd rearranged a few things and had Julian put her valuables in the safe downstairs in his office.

Dread coursed through her. She didn't want to doubt the gift. Julian had never specifically mentioned the coat to her, but why else would he leave something so luxurious in her room if it were not meant for her to use? There was only one other possibility, and a sinking feeling settled over her when she considered it. No one else but Gisele would likely have an interest in the contents of her closet.

Taking a deep breath, Eleni turned off the light in the closet and left the room. In the hallway, she took the servant stairs down to the kitchen, looking for Claudette.

The older housekeeper looked up from scrubbing a copper pot when Eleni entered the room, and tittered loudly. "*Mademoiselle*, you should not be in here. You could ruin your dress."

"I'll only be a minute, I promise. I need you to help me. There was a coat in my closet, a gift from Julian. Do you know where it is?"

"Your coat?" A frown etched Claudette's face. She stopped scrubbing and wiped her hands on the front of her apron. "You're sure it's missing?"

"It isn't where I left it." Eleni chose her words carefully. She doubted Claudette would have much use for a fur coat, and didn't want to make it sound as though she were accusing anyone of theft. Although it seemed the most likely explanation, she didn't want to blame anyone—Gisele, in particular—without proof. But, at the same time, that didn't change the fact the coat was missing, and she wanted to know what had happened to it.

"Come. Let us look for it," Claudette said and bustled from the room. Eleni caught the swinging door on her way through and followed the woman across the entryway. "Not to worry, Mademoiselle. There are only so many places it could be," the housekeeper told her.

She went straight to the coat closet, and opened the door. Eleni stood back as she scraped hangers across the racks.

"*Voila!*" the house keeper declared a moment later, and struggled to work the coat out from the back of the closet and held it up for inspection, smoothing a gnarled, work roughened hand down the front of the fur. "*Zut alors*," the woman said on a breath. "It was far in the back. No wonder you didn't see it." She offered the coat to Eleni. "Perhaps you didn't remember leaving it downstairs."

"That's probably it," Eleni said as she took the coat from Claudette's hands, but she knew that wasn't the case. Only days before she'd taken a coat down from the closet to walk Marguerite from the car. It hadn't been in there at the time. "Do you know where Gisele is, at the moment?"

She shook her head. "Not right off hand. Did you need her for something? It's the weekend, so I would imagine she has gone out with her friends from the village."

"Oh, well, never mind, then. I can catch her later."

"You're sure?"

"It's nothing important," Eleni lied.

"If you say so…" Claudette returned to the closet and began smoothing the coats back in place on the rack. "Are you going out alone this evening, Mademoiselle? Should I call Henri for you?"

"No need for that," Julian said, his voice ringing out from across the foyer.

Eleni turned to see him coming down the stairs, and her heart somersaulted at the vision he made in his black tailored suit.

"I thought we'd have an evening away," he told the housekeeper. "I'm taking her to Gerard's."

Claudette's brows shot up. "This is a surprise." Her mouth drew down, but there was approval shining in her brown eyes. "It will be good for you to get out of the house."

"So I've been told," he teased the housekeeper as he strolled across the foyer to stand beside Eleni. "I'm starting to suspect the two of you are in league."

Claudette cackled. "If that's so, you stand no chance." She winked at Eleni, which made her smile.

"Agreed…" he said as his eyes scanned Eleni from head to toe. Her heart pitter pattered at his heated expression. She could just imagine the effect such a seductive man must've had on society two hundred years ago. Julian probably had women swooning at his feet.

A gentleman to the core, he picked up Eleni's hand and kissed it. "You are a temptation."

Claudette tsked. "You'll make an old woman blush with talk like that." She shut the closet door. "Since I'm no longer needed, I'll go back to my cleaning. A late movie I want to see is coming on at 1:00 AM. I plan to fold clothes while I watch." She turned toward the kitchen, calling back over her shoulder. "Have fun, the two of you. I'll leave the door to the garage unlocked for when you come back."

"Thank you, Claudette," Eleni called after her. Claudette waved a hand over her shoulder in a gesture of friendly dismissal as she bustled away through the swinging door.

"You've charmed her, I see," Julian murmured once they were alone.

"You think so?"

He chuckled. "She is a mother hen, but I love her for it. You're ready to go?"

Eleni nodded, and he took the coat and held it for her while she slid her arms into the satin-lined sleeves. The fur was heavy, and immediately she was enveloped with the ghostly scent of gardenia perfume and cigarette smoke.

Julian frowned. "You're tense. Is something the matter?"

"No. I'm good. I was just thinking…" She shook her head. "It's nothing."

"Whether it's nothing or not, think pleasant things." He cupped her cheek, his thumb caressing her face. "There is just the two of us tonight. I want our time together to be special—and free of any sadness."

Chez Gerard turned out to be a spot of small town elegance in the heart of the Ville Cleménce. The charming plaster and stone building had a dozen slender windows with hunter green trim facing the closed end of the town square, where the clock tower loomed over a large central fountain. Julian told her Chez Gerard's was one of the rare places outside of Bergerac, or pretty much anywhere else in the Périgord Pourpre, that stayed open so late into the evening that they could accommodate vampires.

The menu was written entirely in French, so Eleni had Julian order for her. She told him she wanted to try something that would be considered a local delicacy, and pride had glittered in his gray eyes.

He ordered truffles and grilled trout, along with a bottle of white, Sévigné wine, which Eleni had marveled over, pleasing Julian because she recognized the label at first glance.

"Everything all right with your fish?" Julian asked a short time later.

Eleni looked up at the sound of his voice, but it took her a moment to process what he'd said. She'd been daydreaming, thinking about San Francisco, and the familiar night views of lights glittering in the bay. "Oh." She glanced down at her plate. "Everything's fine, really great. The walnut sauce is amazing."

"That boring, am I?" His voice was droll, teasing, as he swirled wine around in his glass.

"Don't be ridiculous. I'm having a good time, I—" Her breath caught as she stopped, thinking a moment. "You know, this is the first time I've been to the village since I arrived. I suppose I can't help being a little preoccupied."

"I hadn't thought of that," he said absently. "You're right. This is your first evening out." His eyes took on some stormy emotion she had never seen in him before. He took a deep breath. "It must be stifling for you. I don't often leave the chateau for more than business. I wish for your sake I could promise it will not always be this way."

A silence came over him then. A faraway look in his eyes, he stared through the window at the lamp lit square. It hadn't snowed in more than a week, and the snow had mostly melted. Slush remained in the shadowy places along the central median.

"It will be midnight in another thirty minutes or so," he said in a voice that had gone weary. "The restaurant will be closing."

The streets were mostly deserted, yet he stared with a strange, focused intensity out at the night. Eleni could almost see his thoughts working, and thought perhaps he was avoiding some internal battle about his isolation—a topic he didn't seem to want to face, much less discuss.

It hadn't been her intention to make him feel guilty or uncomfortable. It would've been better if she hadn't said anything at all, but it was too late to take it back now. She glanced down at the rare steak on his plate, only partly eaten, enough to give the guise of a human appetite, and her face grew hot. It dawned on her how foolish and dense she had been. Dominic and Marguerite had both told her Julian was reclusive. And why wouldn't he be? He had no need for these kinds of amusements. All of this had been orchestrated for her happiness—the getaway, a night in the village, and dinner in the square.

When he looked at her again, his eyes had gone hard and unreadable. Inside, she withered a little bit. She already missed the warm, open Julian she had come to know—the man who had been sitting right across the table from her until she'd opened her big mouth and ruined the moment.

Although he looked perfectly composed, it occurred to her that this probably wasn't the most comfortable environment for him. He looked dashing in his suit, and his long hair perfectly covered the burn scars along the left side of his neck, but he was a sensitive, self-conscious man.

When they had walked in, he'd attracted the eye of every female, regardless of age, but as a vampire, he still saw himself as tragically flawed.

Her heart went out to him. If she'd thought about it more rationally, she'd never have asked him to bring her here. She took one more bite of grilled fish, savoring the flavor of the delicate seasonings and walnut sauce, then put down her fork. Julian eyed her when she picked up the napkin she'd laid across her lap at the beginning of the meal and dabbed it against her mouth before laying it on the table. "I'm ready to go if you are."

"You're sure? There's still dessert…"

"I'm good…besides, nothing can compare with Claudette's walnut cake."

His eyes glittered with pride. "It would thrill her to hear you say that."

She took another sip of dry white wine while Julian called the waiter over for the bill.

Minutes later, in the tiny tiled entryway, Julian helped her into her coat then held the door for her. An icy wind gusted, whistling around the corners of the stone building, and rattling the front glass as Eleni stepped out onto the cobbled street and waited for Julian, who had turned around to ease the door closed so the wind wouldn't snatch it from his hand and slam it into place.

There were no sidewalks, just a narrow, cobbled road lined with a few cars. Eleni had always liked this time of night, even while living in San Francisco. It seemed cozy and intimate, especially in little places like this. It was quiet and sleepy; most of the humans had gone home, and the walkways were lamp-lit every few feet.

Julian returned to her, and she slipped her arm through his. She took a step toward his car, but he surprised her by steering her in the opposite direction.

She looked up at him. "Where are we going?"

"I thought you might want to see the square before we go home. The traffic is light at the moment, but next week is *la Festival des Masques*. It's an annual street party that takes place throughout the entire village."

"That sounds fantastic!"

"I think you would like it," he said, guiding her in the direction of a large central fountain of a barefoot woman in a flowing skirt with a laurel in her hair. The figure was frozen in a dancer's pose, with one hand clutching her skirts, and the other a tambourine she held in the air.

The water wasn't flowing through it at the moment, but it was impressive all the same. Slushy snow and dried leaves curled in the blacked trough. He let go of her hand and turned a circle, looking around.

"It will not look like this next week. You'll see. I'm usually working when it's going on, but I like to walk through the madness when I can." His grin was devilish. "The revelers wear masks, you see, and there is a street dance with traditional music. The town council holds a pageant and a royal court, and the people who participate spend months on their costumes. There are other entertainments also, such as marionettes, a local art show, and street performers."

"It sounds busy," she said, glancing up at the pointy roofed clock tower directly across from the fountain. It was five minutes until midnight.

"The event is not much different than it was two hundred years ago when it began. I'll take you if I'm not bogged down with work. I think we'd both enjoy it." Silence fell over him before he turned and looked down the square in the direction they'd come from. His expression turned dark, wistful. "It's much the same as it was two hundred years ago, hein? Modernized, of course—the roads are better." He laughed.

Eleni remained silent and allowed him his moment of nostalgia. From the moment she'd first set eyes on him, he had seemed so modern and urbane; it was easy to forget that Julian was several hundred years old. Without a doubt, he had seen many things come and go in his lifetime—roads, buildings, and possibly even entire villages. She could only imagine how it must feel to be surrounded by so much change, only to stumble onto one small area that made you feel, even if only for an instant, that you had been cast back to another time.

A heartbreaking memory from her childhood resurfaced, and an anxious knot tightened in her chest. Almost a year after her mother's death, Eleni had gone into her mother's suite. She had been so confused then, grieving still, and longing for her mother. When she'd entered Ekaterina Audridov's bedroom and shut the door, it had felt a little like walking onto a stage. The silence was perfect. The stillness absolute. Everything about the room had looked normal, exactly as she remembered it. Nothing had been changed or moved.

Feeling like an interloper, she had glanced around the room, almost afraid to move away from the door. Seeing the suite again changed her. It explained everything that up until that point, she had been unable to grasp. Death was about walking into a room and expecting—no, *hoping*—someone you loved would be there. It was permanent absence, despite the tangible things left behind. The things that filled you with heartache and longing for someone you could no longer see or touch.

Standing there quiet and mouse-like, glancing at the mirrored doors of the wardrobe and the mahogany four-poster, everything had seemed so surreal, as if she'd crossed the threshold into a suspended world, one that was neither alive nor entirely departed.

After a few minutes, she had walked over to her mother's dressing table. She looked at the colorful perfume bottles on the gold tray. She saw her mother's favorite red lipstick and pearl combs. Eleni had laid a hand on the handle of her mother's silver hairbrush and was surprised by the coolness of the metal. As if on contact, a sudden haunting emptiness had crawled into her, seizing her lungs, filling her eyes with hot tears.

In that moment, Ekaterina Audridov's essence had seemed strong and all encompassing. So much so, Eleni had half expected her mother to walk through the door at any moment with a loving smile on her face.

A sob caught in Eleni's throat. She turned her back on Julian and pretended an interest in one of the stone buildings before he noticed that tears had sprung to her eyes. Pushing away the vivid memory, she swiped at her tears, feeling pitiful and foolish for crying over it now, especially here in public with Julian. Her mother's passing had happened such a long time ago, but she supposed she'd never fully get over it. Even so, she didn't want to give Julian cause for concern, or ruin their evening together with her tears.

Stress was likely to blame for her sudden loss of control. The threat to her family name still hung over her head, and blending in to Julian's household had not come as easily as she'd hoped it would. Particularly where Gisele was concerned.

"Are you ready to go?" Julian's hand found the small of her back. Eleni clutched at the collar of her fur coat and nodded. If Julian noticed her eyes were wet, he said nothing about it. She was grateful for that.

Together, they walked back down the length of the square in the direction of the restaurant, and were almost to Julian's car when her gaze skittered over two reflective, red orbs in a shadowy throughway between two buildings. She gave a small, involuntary start, but by the time she'd pulled Julian to a stop, whatever she'd seen—whether a vampire's eyes, or a trick of the light—had retreated into the darkness. She laid a hand over her racing heart.

"Did you see that?"

Julian squinted in the direction she indicated. After a moment, he shook his head. "Nothing's there, *mon chou*." He patted her arm and drew her along, but she couldn't keep herself from staring at the shadowy niche across the street.

As Julian walked her to the passenger side door, he pulled the keys from his pocket, and triggered the keyless entry remote to unlock the doors. He shut the door for her, and she reached for the seatbelt. She watched him in the mirror as he rounded the back of the car.

"Hurry, hurry…let's go," she murmured impatiently under her breath. She didn't like the idea of Julian standing out on the street alone, even for a minute.

They rode mostly in silence on the way back to the chateau, Julian driving with a dark expression on his face, and his hand on her knee. They had just reached the vineyard road and were winding their way around the hill when Eleni broke the silence.

"Julian, how many other vampires, besides you and Marguerite, live here in Ville Cleménce?"

"Is this about what you thought you saw in the village?" he said in a level voice. "I told you I saw nothing, but even if some person, or an animal, had been there, they would be no threat to us."

She didn't necessarily agree with that, but she wasn't up for an argument. "That's fine," she said tiredly. "I only glimpsed it for a split second, whatever it was—light, eyes." She shrugged. "I'll take your word for it."

"You have been protected under the banner of the Sévigné name since you arrived at my house. Surely, you know I would never let anyone harm you?"

"I'm grateful for your protection, Julian, but I live here now and I want to know. How many vampires live here?"

Julian's brow furrowed. His let out a deep sigh, and kept his eyes on the road. "No one permanent lives in the area, or I would know about it. There are those who come through on their way to Paris. That's not so unusual. But if someone were to stay for any length of time, it would be considered an insult for the vampire not to announce himself to me, and to Marguerite. This is familial land, after all. It is an old custom, and it is still respected." He was silent for a long moment as he pulled into the private road leading to the front driveway of the chateau. "So, is that it?" he asked. "Is your curiosity satisfied?"

"Yes. Thank you," she said, faintly annoyed with him, and not exactly sure why. Because he didn't believe her? She'd been there herself, he hadn't seen anything, what more could she expect? Nevertheless, as soon as he pulled into an empty space in the garage and parked, she climbed out of the car, slamming the door behind her.

Claudette had left on the light beside the entrance into the dark hall, bless her. The yellow light attracted tiny winged insects that clinked against the glass sconce. Eleni eyed them as she headed toward the door to the windowless passageway, her heels ringing over the cement floor.

Behind her, she heard Julian climb out of the car. He called after her, but she pretended not to hear him. His dismissiveness had embarrassed her and hurt her feelings more than she wanted him to know.

Rubio had made it habit to make her doubt herself, and even though she knew Julian wasn't trying to hurt her in that way, she still wanted to go up to her room and be alone for a while and think. She had seen something, even if she wasn't sure what it was. Maybe it hadn't been vampire eyes, but then again, why not? For all she knew, the vampire council could've hired someone to follow her in France. It was certainly within their power to do so. On top of that, the Elder who'd presided over her case had told her they would be monitoring her progress. Perhaps they had meant more than just discussing her recovery during the probationary hearings.

"Eleni," Julian called after her, his voice echoing in the narrow passageway.

She had almost reached the hidden door Marguerite had showed her, the one with side stairs going up to the west wing of the house, when Julian caught up with her. He caught her by the elbow, his fingers gentle but firm. He turned her to him, and Eleni braced herself for his angry disapproval. Instead, he surprised her by drawing her into his arms and hugging her as if afraid she might vanish into smoke.

He muttered against her hair, words in French that were spoken too quickly and too softly for her to understand. But she felt the emotion in them and her stomach knotted itself into a ball of exquisite tension. She wanted to be a comfort to him. It was more than about duty. He could be as arrogant as any man she had ever met, but she cared about him deeply.

He kissed her temple, then cupped his palm against her cheek and turned her face to his. Their foreheads touched, and his breath fanned coolly against her face. "It wasn't my intention to upset you."

"I know."

"We shouldn't argue—never over such trivial things."

She nodded in agreement, sensing in him some kind of desperation, perhaps the need to connect, to touch. She understood that. It was that kind of connection she'd craved from Rubio, but he had never truly been sincere. Then again, with so many Acolytes living in his house, he didn't have to be. For him, possession was enough—control. Thankfully, Julian was different. He put on a brave front, but even his self-isolation could not free him from emotion. In those moments when he let his guard down, Eleni saw how he struggled with his own heart, and she loved him for it. In her eyes, he was by far a better man than Rubio could ever hope to be.

She reached up and brushed back his midnight hair from his cheek, her heart fluttering when Julian dipped his head and moved his lips over hers in a searing kiss that would have rocked her back on her heels if he hadn't been holding on to her.

Her lips parted, and his tongue dueled with hers, tempted and teased. Eleni reached up and wrapped her arms around him, feeling his hands come under her coat to hold her close to him.

She reveled in his strength, his soothing touch, and the warm amber scent of his cologne, which filled her with feelings of comfort and familiarity. It amazed her that in such a short period of time he had come to represent "home" to her, even though she had no guarantees it would last. For now, that had to be enough. She needed him, more than he could possibly realize.

Julian pulled back to look at her. "We've had a wonderful night up to that point, no?" He picked up her hand and kissed it. "Let us recapture that happiness. We can sit by the fire, enjoy each other's company."

Eleni nodded. "That sounds good to me."

Julian seemed relieved, but as he opened the door to the foyer and held it wide to allow her to enter the house first, his brow furrowed as if something still troubled him. She wondered if it had something to do with their argument, or the possibility that she might have actually seen someone watching them from that dark alleyway in the village.

She didn't know what to think anymore.

Chapter Twelve

Eleni dreamed she was submerged in watery darkness. There was no sound, only a shimmering impression of light somewhere high above her. Lying on her back, she floated comfortably, and didn't become aware that anything was wrong until the light began to shrink away from her.

Panic shot through her, but she couldn't move or even call for help as she sank deeper and deeper into a place of darkness. In her heart, she knew with a certainty that if she didn't regain control and swim for the surface, she was going to die.

Eleni woke up gasping for air, a thin sheet of sweat clinging to her skin. Fear rooted in her chest. She reacted without thought, her hand darting out to her right to find Julian in bed beside her. Relief poured through her when she felt his firm chest beneath her hand. She rolled over to see him sleeping soundly with an arm tossed behind his head.

He looked so comfortable—she didn't want to wake him. Pulling her hand away, she forced herself to get out of bed. After the harrowing dream, she knew she wouldn't be able to go back to sleep right away.

She pulled on a robe and left the room, stepping out into the cool darkness of the east wing. After shutting the door softly behind her, she padded through the quiet hall, and as she rounded the corner into the main corridor, a chill feeling of déjà vu came over her. She stopped short. The dark hallway lightened at the farthest end, reminding her of her dream.

It was around five in the afternoon—the brightness at the end of the corridor came from the last rays of sunlight falling at an angle through the stained glass window. Blurred shapes in red, blue, and green fell broken across the carpet and the balcony railing.

She went downstairs and crossed the foyer to the kitchen, which seemed like a mausoleum without Claudette bustling around in it. She filled a kettle with water and put it on to boil, then went around flipping open cabinets, looking for a cup and saucer, and a tea ball with a chain so she could fill it with tea leaves from the canister by the stove.

Minutes later, she carried her cup of tea to the indoor garden and was about to curl up with her tea on one of the loungers closest to an end table when she noticed movement through the wall of glass, a red fluttering that drew her to a stop.

Her heart gave a frightened leap when she realized someone was standing on the open patio right outside the solarium. Eleni put down her tea and went to the window. She peered through the large leaves of a hothouse palm and to her surprise, saw Claudette and Gisele standing out in the slushy, sun-melted snow, having what was obviously a very heated discussion on the back terrace.

Gisele's red, flutter dress was rumpled, and her hands slashed the air while she talked. Her posture was bent slightly forward as if to hammer home some vital point to Claudette, who stood with her arms crossed, spots of color burning in her sullen cheeks. It must have been important, whatever the argument was about, because Claudette had gone out in a housecoat to take part in it. In all the weeks Eleni had lived with Julian, she had never seen the woman dressed in anything but her serviceable black dress and khaki apron.

Gisele was usually so put together, it was shocking to see her with ratty hair and smudged makeup. She looked as though someone had grabbed her by the neck and given her a good shake.

Claudette kept shaking her head in disapproval until at last Gisele seemed to have had enough. She threw her hands up and shouted angrily at the housekeeper, but the words were muffled through the glass, so Eleni couldn't make out what she said.

Gisele turned toward the house and reached for the door to the solarium, and Eleni jumped in fear. She darted a glance to her left, warily eyeing the cup of tea she'd left steeping on the little side table near the lounger, but it was too late to grab for it without being noticed. She took a step back to shield herself from view, moving behind the elephant ears growing in a cement trough. The glass doors rattled open and Gisele strode into the room, her high heels beating a tattoo over the flagstones. Each staccato note stabbed her nerves.

Claudette was hot on her heels. "You are living an illusion, can't you see that? Who do you think will hurt in the long run? It was the same with Marguerite. Have you not learned your lesson? You can't change the status quo by putting on a red dress."

Claudette tried to take Gisele's hands in hers, but Gisele shook her off.

"You are not my *maman*!"

Claudette looked stricken. Without a doubt, the words had cut her deeply. When she spoke, her voice was low and tremulous. "That doesn't change the fact that this is not what your *maman* would have wanted for you."

"Who the hell are you to know what she would have wanted for me?" Her voice hitched. "I know she didn't want nor expect me to be a servant to anyone."

"That's true. It's why she left. She chose that path for herself. You can't have it both ways, Gisele." Eleni had never seen Claudette look so fierce. Her eyes were over-bright. "Julian won't tolerate it."

"Julian loves me!" Gisele thumped her chest for emphasis. "He confides in me. If not for her, I would be his lover."

The fine hairs prickled on the back of Eleni's neck.

Again, Claudette shook her head. "We aren't meant to be with the vampires in such a way. You know this. You were raised knowing this, Gisele. Such a fantasy goes against everything we stand for. It's dangerous—"

"You're afraid of them," Gisele accused angrily. "Just like maman was afraid." Her mouth trembled. "She was beautiful and dedicated. She could have been so much more than a servant."

"Childish daydreams," Claudette burst out. "Your mother knew her place. She never would have attempted what you are doing—playing a fool's game. But what else could I expect? You are a foolish girl—you have always been foolish."

Gisele struck her, a sharp slap that rang out, echoing through the cavernous garden. Utter silence followed it. The fountain gurgled, a quiet rushing noise that seemed to amplify the tension in the room. Eleni's heart galloped. She watched in disbelief, riveted, both hands over her mouth.

Claudette reeled, her mouth agape. A heavy hand came up and pressed itself to her reddened cheek. Her breathing had gone ragged as she stared into Gisele's face, which had whitened perceptibly.

Finally, Gisele turned on her heel and strode from the room. Claudette stood watching her until the click-clack of Gisele's high heels grew distant and faded. Several heartbeats later, Claudette followed her out of the room.

Eleni remained in her hiding spot behind the leaves, processing this startling new threat, afraid to move, afraid to stay in case someone returned to the solarium. Gisele's dislike of her had taken on an ominous new meaning, especially where Julian was concerned, and she didn't know what to do about it.

Claudette was right about one thing. While Julian had fostered Gisele, he would never consider making her an Acolyte, much less a bloodmate. It was taboo, especially in aristocratic circles, and Julian was too old fashioned, too much of a traditionalist to break that unspoken code, even if he often claimed that he didn't care what the council thought of his actions.

Still, it worried her that Gisele thought otherwise. The girl had already threatened her once. When she was sure no one was coming back to the garden, Eleni went to the end table and picked up her teacup and saucer. The tea was cold in the cup and had over-steeped, but she didn't want to risk leaving it behind, or carrying it back to the kitchen. Instead, she poured it out into one of the plant troughs and left the garden, careful to avoid running into anyone on the way up to her room.

The following Wednesday, after making love to Julian in the shower, Eleni had wrapped herself in a towel and sprawled out on Julian's bed while he faced the closet mirror and dressed in a pair of black trousers and a crisp white shirt. Contented and languorous, she stretched out on her side, admiring him, until she realized he was putting on a tie. It was then he told her he had to go to Bergerac to discuss business with his primary accountant, and would be gone for most, if not all, of the night. Henri was to drive him, and he would likely be back sometime near dawn, but on the event he had to get a hotel there, he would call her before he slept.

Feeling deflated, and anxious about staying in the house without him, Eleni stuck with him like a shadow until at last Henri arrived around eight o'clock. At the front door, Julian kissed her goodbye, promising to bring her back a trinket from one of the shops. She had fixed a smile to her face, even though she didn't feel it, even though she couldn't care less about gifts, or trinkets. If he didn't make it back before dawn, it would be the first time she had slept alone since her arrival at the house. She had no idea what she'd do without him around.

Some two hours later, after the car had pulled out of the drive, she was still feeling let down. The chateau was a nowhere place without Julian—too large, too impersonal.

She took her laptop computer down to the small parlor and checked the news, the stock market, and was curled up on the couch writing an email to Anya when she heard a light rap on the facing of the open doorway. She looked up, and over the rim of her glasses, saw Claudette in the doorway, concern in her dark eyes.

"Claudette?"

"*Mademoiselle.*" The housekeeper stepped into the room and presented a tall, pale gentleman with reddish brown hair. "Liev Sidorov from the vampire council is here to see you."

Eleni sat up and shut the lid of her laptop. When her eyes landed on the man coming in through the door, her heart leapt with sudden wary fear. For an instant, her lungs seized and her brain froze. *It can't be. He wouldn't come here.* The thought whirled in her head, tormented in those few seconds before he stepped forward out of the shadows and she got a good look at him.

She almost cried out in relief when she realized the man wasn't who she thought he was, but the likeness was remarkably similar. In fact, he looked so much like Zander Rubio, her ex-Biter, she felt instantly threatened by his presence.

He came toward her with an easy stride and introduced himself in heavily accented English. The words seem to soar right over her head, but after the initial shock had worn off, she saw it was merely the angle of his jaw and his coloring that made this vampire look so much like her ex-lover. This Liev Sidorov made a passable imposter, but he would never compare with Zander's exquisite handsomeness. His nose was too pointed and too narrow, his forehead too high.

Still, his appearance was enough to rattle her. Eleni stood up to offer him a chilly greeting, and in exchange, he offered her the tiniest of bows.

"I apologize for dropping in on you unannounced, Miss Audridov," he said, his accent crisp and distinctly Russian. Eleni fixed on his fangs when he spoke, then flicked a glance over to Claudette, who stood waiting. She had no intention of speaking to him unless she was alone.

"My Biter isn't home. Should I have my housekeeper call him for you?"

"Ah, no, no… There's no need." He glanced briefly over his shoulder at Claudette. "It isn't my intention to take up much of your time. May we talk in private?"

Eleni hesitated, but decided at last she would. "Thank you, Claudette. Could you close the door on your way out, please?"

"Should I bring anything, madam? Wine, perhaps?"

"That won't be necessary," she said without consulting her 'guest'. Eleni had a feeling Julian wouldn't have been thrilled to know she was entertaining a vampire without his supervision, but she very well couldn't send him away without hearing what he had to say first. She could ill afford to rile the council. There were enough grievances against her already. That did not mean she intended to make Mr. Sidorov feel comfortable enough to stay longer than was absolutely necessary.

Claudette nodded sharply, glancing one last time at the vampire before backing out of the room. The door closed softly behind her, and only then did Eleni turn her attention to the councilman, whom she regarded with a mixture of confusion and contempt.

"May I sit down?" he asked, gesturing to a seat. Eleni permitted it with a turn of her hand, and while he settled himself into Julian's chair, she sat down in her own chair and addressed him in Russian in case anyone tried to eavesdrop on their conversation.

"I'm surprised to see a member of the council so soon," she said, roiling in her dislike of him. "I wasn't told I'd receive house visits, and I know I'm not up for review until May. The way I was told, I'd have to travel with my Biter to Paris to face the review board there."

"I know this probably seems like an unwelcome intrusion on your new life. However, I must confess that's not why I'm here—to judge you in any way." Even as he said it, something hidden danced in his eyes, which were a shade of hazel brown so light they were almost the exact same shade as his auburn hair. "I think you know there are at least a few Elders who would like to see your name stricken from the Book of Acolytes."

Eleni tensed. "Are you threatening me?" She didn't try to hide the sharpness of her voice.

Immediately, the glimmer of sly amusement vanished. He sat straighter, his mouth drawn down at the corners. "I'm offering you a deal, a chance to clear your name with the council, and move on with your life. Isn't that what you want?"

Chill warning scraped through her. "My brother-in-law is well connected. I highly doubt you could offer me anything he couldn't arrange with the council himself."

"Ah, but that's not true. It's politics, you understand. You are from a very distinguished line. Think about that. Whatever affects you, also affects you sister—who I hear is a charming vampiress now that she has turned."

He pulled out a thin sheaf of bundled pages from the inside pocket of his jacket and unfolded them.

"Rubio sent you?" The question came out tense and bitter. She already knew the answer. "He must be desperate if he sent you all the way to France to hound me."

"The council was harsh with him, as they were with you."

"So you're some kind of representative?" By the look of him, a relative was probably more like it.

"If you agree and sign this, Rubio is willing to take responsibility for your condition before the council, and he'll pay you a settlement to satisfy the damage done to your family name. In return, you must exonerate him, of course. Sign a letter of forgiveness that will be sent to Grigori Vidam for his approval. By signing this statement, you tell the court you forgive Rubio of his part in your illness. The council will have no choice but to honor the agreement."

His proposal galled her. Rubio had put her through absolute hell and now he wanted her to sign papers so he could have a lighter sentence levered against him. She knew the conditions of his punishment had been weighed against him based on the years of abuse he'd put her through. "You both must be out of your minds."

The vampire looked momentarily taken aback. His lips thinned. "I assure you, much thought has been put into this."

She scoffed. "Oh, I don't doubt that."

"Zander's lawyers have worked tirelessly to find a loophole."

Just like that, his expression hardened into an unreadable mask. "It would save you both going through an appeal that the council has neither the time nor the inclination to deal with."

"I think you should leave." She stood up and walked to the door. "You tell Rubio I plan to report this offer to the council. If he approaches me again, I'll have Julian call him out. Do you hear me?"

Slowly, the vampire stood up. Eleni watched him drop the sheaf of papers gently onto the coffee table before making his way around the furniture to leave.

When he reached the doorway, he stopped in front of her and stared into her eyes. Eleni swallowed hard. She was tall, but Liev Sidorov towered over her by almost a full foot. Without saying a word, he reached into his coat pocket and extracted a business card. He handed it to her.

Eleni reluctantly slipped it from his fingers. She looked down at it, and saw his name embossed in black letters. The number and address was to a suite in Paris.

"It's hardly an olive branch, but I hope you'll put aside your anger and consider what is being offered to you. You know already the council is biased against you. The stigma of Biter's Addiction isn't something that goes away with time. If it isn't stricken from the record purposely, it will haunt your bloodline for generations. You don't want that. I know you don't, or you wouldn't be in France. Rubio wants to be free, so much so he's willing to brush off his wounded pride to offer freedom to his enemy in order to attain it. Agree to this. Sign the papers and the past will go away for both of you."

"Goodbye, Liev Sidorov." Her voice wavered with barely restrained anger. His eyes gleamed, sly and brimming with dislike. "If even one of your probationary reviews goes wrong, you could find yourself cast out of vampire society. Neither Julian nor Dominic will be able to help you then. Where will you go? How will you live?"

She was smart enough to recognize his veiled threat. Her pulse quickened, but she held herself in check. It would be dangerous to show weakness. Without a doubt, he would report just such a finding back to Rubio, and she knew her ex-Biter wouldn't hesitate to exploit her fears.

Their eyes locked in silent challenge. At last, Eleni broke the silence, switching seamlessly from the vampire's native Russian to English. "Should I call Claudette to show you out?"

"That won't be necessary." He bid her a brusque goodnight and left.

Eleni stood in the doorway for several minutes, her nerves jangling, her breathing harsh and ragged. Her eyes lingered on the contract he'd left on Julian's coffee table as though the file itself held a dangerous life of its own.

The vampire's footfalls rang down the hallway, fading, growing distant. Her heart cried with relief when she heard the front door open and close as he let himself out. Turning, she padded quickly through the house to the foyer. Standing at one of the slender windows along either side of the front door, she watched the vampire get into a shiny black car with darkly tinted windows. A moment later, the lights came on, and the car crunched over the white rock as it pulled out of the driveway.

"Is everything all right, Mademoiselle?"

Eleni looked over her shoulder at Claudette. The woman stood in the doorway to the kitchen with her hands clenched together in her apron. Her face was lined with worry.

Uncertain, she took a deep breath and shook her head. "I hope, but… I don't know."

Chapter Thirteen

Around 9:00 PM the following night, Julian and Henri returned from their business trip to Bergerac. Upstairs in her room, Eleni had just gotten out of the shower and was getting dressed in jeans and a black blouse when she heard the car pull up in the driveway. Her hair wrapped in a towel, she went to the window. Henri had parked Julian's black sedan directly in front of the house, and while Eleni watched, absently rubbing her hair with the towel, one of the doors opened, and Julian climbed out of the car and stretched.

Excitement burst through her, joy and relief. Glad he was home, she couldn't wait to talk to him, to hold him. She dropped the curtain and the towel, and left her room, padding barefoot through the house to greet her Biter.

She met him in the entryway as he was shuffling in through the front door carrying department store shopping bags. He looked disheveled, but incredibly sexy.

"I'm glad you're home!" Eleni said as she darted forward and hugged Julian. He returned her embrace, crinkling shopping bags. Laughter rumbled in his chest.

"Is it safe to believe you missed me?" His eyes gleamed with happiness as he eyed her wet hair and kissed her on the tip of the nose. "This one is for you," he told her, and handed her a striped shopping bag, which was fairly heavy. He also had bags for Claudette and Gisele.

"So, what's this?" Eleni asked and started to poke through the bag, but Julian stilled her with an amused chuckle.

"You might want to save that until we go to my office."

She blinked at him. "Oh?"

"You should trust me on this."

Her brows lifted at the wicked smile on his face. Now she was more curious than ever, but before she could ask what he'd been up to, Henri entered the house behind him, looking withered and exhausted. "I'll be happy to sleep in my own bed again," he grumbled, and an amused look crossed Julian's face.

Claudette peeked out of the kitchen. "Ah, so there you are. It was a good trip?"

"We made it out alive," Henri said tiredly on his way across the foyer to her. "You have coffee made, no? Help an old man, will you, Claudie?"

Her mouth drew into a perfect moue. "I suppose I could do that."

Claudette turned to go back into the kitchen with Henri, but Julian caught the housekeeper before she could slip away and gave her a small gift bag. The woman's face lit up as she peeked into the bag, rustling the tissue. "My favorite chocolate," she said, beaming. She came over and gave Julian a hearty kiss on both cheeks.

There was no sign of Gisele. Julian said nothing about her absence, merely guided Eleni back to his office. While he stripped off his wristwatch and cufflinks and tossed them onto his desk, Eleni told him about the vampire that had come by the house.

"What was his name?" Julian flipped through the contract she'd left on his desk while she struggled to remember.

"He left a card. It's there on your desk," she told him. "The last name was Sidorov. A fairly common name, I think. I had a ballet teacher with the same surname once. She had no relationship to any vampires, of course, but's how I remember it. Anyway, I'd recognize him if I saw him again."

"You're sure of that?"

"Quite sure." She nodded, then described the vampire in detail. What she didn't tell Julian was that the man had looked a lot like her ex-Biter. She didn't want him to jump to any conclusions about why she'd found a strange vampire so memorable.

"I will contact the council about it and find out what's going on. I've heard of them sending people out to conduct similar duties—that's not so uncommon, but usually there is at least some notice, even if only a day in advance." He flopped down in his office chair and sighed. "But never mind all that, I want you to open your gift."

"Well, I know it's not a puppy," she teased.

Julian pulled her into his lap, kissed her shoulder, and toyed with her long hair while she fished through the bag, rattling the tissue paper. She stopped when she reached his gift—or rather, gifts. "Well... Interesting."

He leaned his head back and watched her surprised reaction through hooded eyes. "Is that a declaration of approval?"

Eleni leaned over and gave him a kiss, which he greeted with opened-mouthed lust. He caught her chin with his fingers, urged her to kiss him more thoroughly, intimately. Her tongue slid against his, while his hand slid from her shoulder to her breast, then to her thigh and squeezed.

She raked her teeth over her lower lip, felt the start of an impressive bulge in the front of his pants. With her hand, she reached out idly and caressed it, kneading through the fabric of his trousers.

"Mm," she murmured huskily. "I hope you didn't get Gisele the same gift."

"No worries about that," he said, and brushed her hair back from her shoulder. Then he fascinated himself with the buttons of her blouse, before parting the fabric and settling his interest on the mounds of her bare breasts.

Julian kissed her temple, his fingers pinching and tweaking her sensitive nipples into hard nubs. "Which color do you want in your pussy first? The green one? Blue?"

It was a tough call. Instead of trying to decide by sight, she rooted in the bag and chose at random, selecting by touch. From the bag, she withdrew a pale purple vibrator. Silver glitter sparkled in the silicone. Judging by the look in Julian's eyes, he approved.

She leaned back against him, allowing him access to the button and zipper of her jeans. Julian worked the fastenings and stroked the crotch of her jeans before sliding his hand down the front of her jeans, past the thin barrier of her panties.

He teased her clit until she squirmed on his lap.

"It feels good?" he asked, his voice a hoarse whisper.

Eleni nodded, "Very."

Julian kissed her again, working his fingers in a slow, sensual exploration of her silky pussy lips and tight, hot hole. His fingers rubbed her swollen clitoris, flicking and teasing. Eleni's pussy throbbed with need and her inner thighs were slicked with wetness.

Once he had her wet enough, Julian urged her off of his lap. He leaned forward to help her out of her shirt, jeans, and panties, then reached for the gift bag and extracted a bottle of vanilla-scented oil.

He massaged oil along her slit, slid a finger deep inside her then slowly added another.

Julian's cock was fully erect, jutting against the fabric of his black trousers. Eleni reached down and freed his belt buckle, button, and zipper, allowing his hard, hot flesh to spill forward. He kicked off his shoes under the desk, lifted his hips, and eased out of his pants. Taking the bottle of oil, he stood up, picked up Eleni's hand, and pooled the fragrant oil in her palm.

"Stroke me."

Eleni did as he bid of her. She wrapped her hands around his cock and massaged the oil into the velvet skin. Her hands made slick noises over his flesh. Julian sighed with pleasure. His gray eyes had grown hazy with lust. She cupped his balls, gently slicked his sac with her thumbs until it puckered tight and glistened.

Eyes hungry with lust, he urged her to sit on the edge of the desk, and splayed her thighs with a touch of his hand. Cool air touched her pussy and made her shiver, her nipples puckering in response.

Julian stroked his hands over the insides of her thighs, slid her legs apart and rubbed her clit with his fingers, moistening her pussy with the scented lubricant. He then picked up the vibrator she'd chosen and twisted the black base until the toy hummed.

The buzzing hum seemed to vibrate right to the core of her, to her bones. He slid it through her wet folds in slow torment, then massaged her tender clitoris before tracing her folds again and delving deep. Eleni moaned and arched her back, welcoming the penetration. She tilted her hips to put pressure against the curved head of the toy and rolled her body, savoring the sweet sensations that curled through her.

"Like that, do you?" Julian murmured, his eyes blazing with sensual heat. He slid the vibrator in and out, fucking her with it until he finally buried it deep enough that the silicone bud along the side of the toy rested against her swollen clitoris. The vibrator buzzed inside her, the swirling head of the clitoral stimulant made her breathing shallow.

"Oh, God," Eleni groaned, her eyelids slipping to half-mast. "I'm…Oh, Julian, it feels so good…"

Julian tugged her forward so her legs hung off the desk. Guiding her with his hands, he turned her around, urging her hand between her legs to hold the toy in place. While he moved in behind her with the oil, he told her she made a gorgeous sight, fucking herself with the vibrator he'd bought for her.

Swirling sweet sensation hit her in all the right places. Eleni was thoroughly turned on, ready to take Julian's cock in her ass when he added more lubrication to her sensitive rosette. With the toy buried deep inside her pussy, he levered his cock against her asshole and pressed slowly forward, sinking into her depths with a guttural moan.

Eleni flinched only a moment as the head of his cock penetrated, nudging deep. She cried out softly as her stomach muscles clenched, which made her muscles squeeze him tight. But with the steady stimulation of the vibrator buzzing her tender clitoris, she soon found herself melting around the thickness of his hard cock. Her whole body was pulsing with desire, with the need to come.

Gasping with every stroke of his cock, she lowered her head, fingers clenching the vibrator with one hand, the desk blotter with the other. Lost in ecstasy, her eyes slipped shut and she panted. She felt so full, so completely filled by his cock and the vibrator. He rocked inside her, gasping loudly as he pumped his cock in and out. She knew he felt the vibration of the toy through her walls, even while buried deep in her ass. She saw his face reflected in the silver ball paperweight on his desk. Despite the distorted image, his eyes were hot with pleasure.

"Ah yes, ah…Eleni…you're so tight I can hardly bear it." His husky confession shot excitement through her. He varied his speed while he fucked her, slow for a while, then fast, but every stroke penetrated her deliberately and deep.

A fine sheen of sweat broke over her body as chills spread across her skin. His fingers toyed with her breasts, tweaking and torturing her erect nipples. The plucking motions made her inner walls contract so that she squeezed both him and the toy.

It was sensory overload—one moment too little, the next too much. Rippling pleasure started deep in some secret core of her. She felt it rolling forward, pushing its way up through her body, shivering along nerve endings until it erupted in overwhelming pleasure that tore an ecstatic breath from her lips.

Her heartbeat pounded in her ears as the tide of erotic sensation crashed over her, shook her down into pools of melted pleasure. Leaning over her, he scraped his fangs against her shoulder blade and murmured softly to her. He told her how beautiful she was, how perfect her breasts felt in his hands, how the smooth glide of her asshole teased him when she flexed her inner walls so that they gripped his cock.

Sparks shot through her, high and sweet, nearly overwhelming. A sharp cry escaped her lips as inescapable pleasure wracked her body in delicious waves.

"Ah, yes," he ground out, his voice ragged. The walls of her pussy fluttered around him, and he laid his head back, closing his eyes, focusing on the sensation. On the brink, he began to groan. Sweating, breathing hard, he gripped her hips, fucked her in hard, furious strokes that made her body lunge with the every forceful thrust of his cock. "My sweet angel…so wet and willing, such a good fuck."

His words drifted away into a string of nonsense and filth praise muttered through a tide of lust until finally his body quickened, his thrusts became jerky, irregular. He erupted with a guttural moan, his come filling her in hot spurts as bliss wracked his body.

He held himself inside her until he'd spent his last, then withdrew. Eleni pulled the toy away, and weak with satisfaction, turned it off. Julian reached for her and pulled her down onto his lap as he eased back into the desk chair. For a long time they sat there, holding one another, caressing each other absently until their breathing returned to normal.

After several minutes, Eleni smiled up at him in hazy satisfaction. "So I take it you missed me while you were away?"

He kissed her shoulder. "More than anything."

* * *

Toward dawn, Eleni pulled on her jeans and rumpled shirt while Julian straightened his office. He stood at the wet bar and washed and dried Eleni's new toys and put them back into the gift bag so they could be carried upstairs discreetly.

They were just about to go upstairs together when Julian's desk phone rang. Cursing under his breath, he hesitated at the gate of the elevator. It rang again and he let out a resigned sigh. "I better answer it."

Eleni sighed softly, waiting near the gate, hoping the call wouldn't take long.

Julian reached the desk in two strides and halted with his hand on the phone. He had noticed the gift bag still on the edge of his desk and gestured to it as he lifted the phone from the cradle. "Eleni, could you take this to Gisele's room, please? Leave it on her bed?" He tucked the phone to his ear, "Hello?" Then, covering the mouthpiece with the heel of his hand, he spoke quietly to her. "I will meet you upstairs."

Contempt flared up in her, but she bit it down, held it back. Regardless of how she felt about Gisele, it was hardly an unreasonable request.

Eleni knew where Gisele's room was, although she had never gone that far down the eastern corridor before. There had never been any reason to seek her out until now, and since that night she'd found the woman trying on her clothes, she had made it a point to avoid her as much as possible.

With Julian already on the phone, she took the gift and left the office, closing the door behind her. She paused outside the door and peeked into the bag, curious, because the gift was slightly heavy. Poking through the tissue paper, she saw it was a figurine of a black poodle with green gem eyes, something you'd give to a sister, or maybe a child.

Eleni puzzled over that until she reached the end of the hall and cut across the marble foyer, which felt cold as ice on her bare feet. Claudette had already dimmed the lights, and the house seemed filled with shadows and a cryptic silence.

On her way past the small parlor, she glanced left into the room where Zander's representative had threatened her. A tremor of unease skittered through her. The gas fireplace was now a dark cavern at the far end of the room, blocked off by a gold, fan-shaped screen that glinted in the shadows.

By now, Claudette had gone to bed, and Henri had likely returned to his gîte. Alone in this part of the house felt strange and uncomfortable, as if it were a separate entity from the rest of the house and she didn't belong here. Walking down the carpeted corridor, she glanced at the paintings lining the walls, dozens of them, some of them quite old.

There were eerie red sunsets, crows, Madonna and child, the vineyard at harvest, and bottles of wine with baskets of grapes and cheese. In each painting, the brushstrokes seemed to capture centuries of thought in mottled colors that made Eleni think of ancient despair.

A chill raced over her skin as she reached the corner and turned to her right. Immediately, the bedroom door came into view. Eleni walked to the door and stopped. She reached up to knock but hesitated. She was inexplicably nervous. It wasn't like the woman could kill her or anything.

Still, dread curled through her as she was reminded of all those times she'd thought about peeking in on Gisele's room, wondering what it might reveal about her, what sort of a glimpse it might offer into her psyche, perhaps. At the same time, she feared it might tell her things she didn't want to know, or in some way confirm or at least make sense of her concrete belief that Julian loved her. If there was any proof to the claim, certainly there had to be evidence of it in that bedroom.

It worried her, what she would say if she ran into her. Eleni wasn't afraid of her, exactly, but the anticipation of weathering her unpleasantness was enough to make her heart race. She didn't think Gisele was home, but when she stopped in front of the bedroom door, she hesitated before knocking.

She rapped twice against the pocket door and waited. There was no answer. She started to knock again, but at the last second, halted, considering. Glancing back over her shoulder, she assured herself she was alone in the hallway and slipped her hand around the door handle and pressed the latch with her thumb. The door wouldn't budge.

Oh, really?

Eleni tried again, rattling the door, but it was locked. Slow anger crept through her, a blistering crimson heat that settled in her face.

"There are no locked doors. No secrets in my house."

Apparently that rule didn't apply to Gisele. Or more likely, it did, but Gisele blatantly disregarded it, and Julian was blissfully unaware of that fact. Eleni imagined there was probably quite a bit going on under Julian's nose without his knowledge, particularly where Gisele was concerned.

Eleni hung the straps of the bag over the doorknob, hoping that when Gisele found it, she took it for the message that it was. *I've got figured you out.*

Not only did Gisele lock her door, Eleni hadn't seen her in the house since her argument with Claudette in the garden. Deep in thought, she walked back down the dark corridor toward the foyer.

As she gripped the rail and started upstairs to her room, she wondered where Gisele had been going almost every evening. Claudette said Gisele had friends in the village, but if that were true, they must be questionable friends, because Gisele hadn't once mentioned anyone by name, or brought them to the chateau to visit, not even in passing.

She had to be spending the daylight hours somewhere. Either Julian hadn't noticed, or didn't care that his servant went missing for days at a time. When she considered how much Gisele disliked her, it made her feel like she was living under constant threat. No wonder Julian liked transparency.

As much as the double standard annoyed her, Eleni had no plans to get in an argument over it as long as Gisele kept her distance. Her upcoming probationary hearing and Rubio's vampire representative gave her enough to worry about without Gisele's secret life—both inside and outside the chateau—adding to it.

Chapter Fourteen

"I want you to go," Julian told Eleni as he rummaged through the papers on his desk. For the past half hour, he'd been frantically getting things in order for the wine distributor who had called unexpectedly earlier in the evening and was now on his way to the chateau from Bergerac to discuss plans for the new Sévigné vintage.

She understood the importance of this meeting, and hated to bother him when he was so obviously busy and distracted as he was at the moment, but when he'd called her down to his office to cancel their planned outing, she thought that was the end of it. She hadn't expected him to make other arrangements for her.

"Julian, the whole point of going to the festival was to go with you."

"I don't want you to miss it on my behalf." He glanced up from his desk and papers to gaze at her with a faraway look in his eyes. He moved to the filing cabinet across the room and began to dig through a drawer. "I don't know why you're so reluctant to go. I've already talked to Gisele about it, and she agreed to drive you. The two of you can go together and take in the sights. It's not like it's a hardship. She'd already planned to go herself."

Not a hardship, Eleni thought with derision. If only he knew. It was the first night of *Le Festival Des Masques*, and while she'd been excited about it and wanted to go in the beginning, she'd changed her mind the minute she'd learned Julian expected Gisele to take her in his place. Dread churned in her stomach when she imagined herself stranded with Gisele's sour attitude for the night.

She folded her arms across her chest and sighed. "I think I'd rather just stay home and watch TV."

"And have you sulking on me later that you never go anywhere?" He grunted his disapproval.

"When have I ever done that?"

"You haven't—yet. And that's the point."

Annoyed, Eleni watched him pick up a stack of printed pages off his desk. He tapped the loose ends into place on the blotter before shoving everything into a desk drawer. Of course, Gisele wouldn't tell Julian no to a request to act as a chaperone in the village. That didn't mean the woman wanted to spend the evening showing her around—and as far as Eleni was concerned, the feeling was mutual, festival be damned.

She was just about to tell him that when a sudden sharp knock on the door had her glancing back over her shoulder. Julian stilled, cursing under his breath. He still wasn't prepared. The rapping started up again, leaving him no choice but to round his desk and head for the door.

Observing quietly, Eleni backed up toward the sitting area, her arms folded firmly across her chest while he went to the door and opened it.

Claudette stood in the hallway. "The man from Bergerac has arrived," she informed him quietly.

"Send him in, please, Claudette. Oh, and could you make coffee?"

The housekeeper nodded, her eyes drifting toward Eleni before she backed out of the room and shut the door. When she was gone, Julian took a deep breath to relieve tension before he crossed the room and pulled Eleni into an embrace.

"You'll give me no trouble tonight, *hein*?"

She wrapped her arms low around his waist, sighing, resigned to do what she really didn't want to do if it satisfied him. It was her job to please him, after all, and he seemed to want this adventure for her, whatever the reason. She lowered her eyes, but it didn't stop him from kissing the tip of her nose, then her forehead. At last, he lifted her chin and forced her to look at him.

"I know you're disappointed. I said I would take you— now this." He brushed a stray lock of blond hair from her cheek. "Don't look so down. It can't be helped."

"I know…it's not that."

"I promise to make this up to you. Now go with Gisele. Have a good time." He held her at arm's length then kissed her hand as he moved away to the office door, where someone now knocked—Claudette with the business man.

Frowning at no one, Eleni thought grimly of the night ahead and turned, walking across the room to take Julian's private elevator up to the second floor.

By nine-thirty, Eleni had showered and dressed in sweater, jeans, and a comfortable pair of riding boots, since she expected to do a lot of walking. Standing in front of her dresser mirror, she applied her makeup, and braided her long hair into a single plait, knowing the whole time she was dragging her feet and only putting off the inevitable.

Finally, she grabbed her wallet and her keys, resigned to the fact she wouldn't be able to excuse her way out of this situation. On her way downstairs, she tried to convince herself the evening could turn out passable, if not okay.

From the foyer, she heard the car running out front. She went to the coat closet and took down a navy pea coat and slipped it on over her shoulders, bracing herself for the worst.

Outside, the evening air was chilly and slightly damp. A thin white mist rose up from the vineyard, which began down the hill from Julian's house. She quickly crossed the raked gravel drive and climbed into the waiting car. As she strapped on her seatbelt, she glanced over at Gisele, who sat mutely behind the wheel, her dark eyes glittering with barely restrained dislike. That, along with the angry set of her jaw, told Eleni everything she needed to know. *Yeah, this is going to be fun. A real picnic!*

They spoke barely two words to one another all the way to Ville Cleménce, and that suited Eleni just fine. But as they reached the edge of the village and Gisele began navigating their way through traffic-choked streets, Eleni began to feel overwhelmed by it all—the crowds of people, the loud music, and anonymous mask-covered faces of hundreds of strangers.

Julian hadn't been kidding when he'd claimed the festival was a major local attraction. Street vendors had cropped up everywhere and were selling everything under the moon, from food to balloons, to collectibles and trinkets. Almost everyone wore, or at least carried, a silk or paper mask.

Gisele navigated the traffic well. Even so, Eleni was relieved when she began looking for a place to park. Keeping to the side streets, Gisele stayed away from the immediate action, and kept hunting in areas that wouldn't put them too far away from the square to walk.

Eleni was relieved when they came across the glowing red taillights of a car pulling out of a tight parking space. Gisele rushed up the street to stake her territory then hung back to wait for the car to vacate the spot. Horns blared behind them. Gisele looked up into the rearview mirror, agleam of reflected light created a skewed rectangle across her face. Cursing the impatient drivers under her breath, she weathered the annoying insults that were hurled at them and refused to budge.

Eleni didn't realize how hard she was gripping the edge of her seat until Gisele zipped into the empty spot. She killed the engine, and finally, Eleni was able to relax.

A humorless laugh escaped her lips. "I'm glad you were the one driving. I'd have turned back at the edge of town." She looked across at Gisele, reaching out, hopeful. She lowered her voice a fraction, testing the waters. "I think we can manage to get along for one night, don't you?"

Gisele scoffed as though the very idea was an insult. Her smoky eyes brimmed with malice as she flicked her gaze over Eleni's face. "I told Julian I'd bring you here, but I never agreed to be your babysitter."

Just like that, she snatched her leather handbag from the center console and got out of the car, slamming the door behind her. Stunned, Eleni gaped after her then hurried to get out of the car. By the time she set foot on the street, Gisele was already a half a block down the street, walking with an arrogant jauntiness that rapidly ate up the distance.

Eleni started after her, following the woman's blonde head of hair through a thin crowd that walked along the narrow strip, but then up the block, a car came slowly around the corner, turning onto the street in her direction with the headlights beaming brightly.

Eleni squinted in the brightness and lifted her hand to shield her eyes before the car passed. In that short amount of time, she completely lost sight of Gisele.

Worry swirled through her as she walked to the end of the block. At the corner, she stood beneath the street lights while looking around at the vendors and the shops, searching for any sign of Gisele among the people drifting by and finding none.

She wondered briefly whether to go back to the car and wait. But then her anger caught up with her. If Gisele thought she was going to let this one slide, she was in for a rude awakening.

Falling in behind a group of pedestrians, two nice looking young couples trailing woolen scarves and carrying stick masks, Eleni made up her mind to explore. A determined scowl crossed her face. If she ended up lost, with no other choice but to hire a driver to take her back to the chateau, so be it. She'd let Gisele explain that one to Julian.

Two hours later, she wandered around the bustling village square. It had taken her a few false turns to find it, but once she did, her anxiety eased and she began to enjoy herself. A temporary stage had been set up near the fountain where Julian had walked with her weeks before. The fountain gurgled with water now, and a local band complete with accordions, clarinets, and a piccolo played a traditional French song to a masked, enthusiastic crowd. The melody was so moody and haunting it seemed to shiver through the night air like an electric current.

Eleni listened to it, the hairs prickling along the back of her neck. She kept glancing around, expecting to find Gisele at any minute, but there was still no sight of her. She stopped to watch a part of a marionette show and had just finished eating a chocolate crepe she'd bought from a street vendor, when she turned to walk back toward the an area closer to the stage that had places to sit. She walked head-first into another woman and would have toppled to the ground if the woman hadn't caught her up and steadied her.

"Oh, God, I'm so sorry," Eleni blurted in English.

"Eleni, it's me!" The woman laughed as if it were all a great joke, and Eleni straightened, red-faced, relieved to see Marguerite's familiar face beaming at her in amusement. Before Eleni could say a word, Marguerite greeted her with a brief kiss on both cheeks. Then, she glanced around as if searching for someone. "This is such a pleasant surprise. Julian is with you?"

"No. I came with Gisele…who is somewhere around here."

"Abandoned you, did she?" The vampiress didn't sound surprised. "The girl is insolent. No respect for others, or for her station in life," she said with a sniff. "But never mind her; I was just going to this little café to sit and watch the crowds. I'm old, you know?" Her eyes twinkled with mischief. "I've been shopping and I need to rest my feet. You must come with me."

Marguerite led her to a sidewalk café not far from the restaurant where she and Julian had dined only days before. They found an empty table and claimed it. Marguerite sat down heavily in one of the chairs and dropped her shopping bags by her feet.

"*Zut*! Let us sit for a while to catch our breath. I don't know about you, but I've been up since before the sun went down." She waved to a passing waiter, catching him before he disappeared into the building. "*Monsieur, deux cafés, s'il vous plaît.*"

The man nodded and turned away. Marguerite looked back around at Eleni. "Coffee is good?"

"Yes, thank you."

Marguerite's brow furrowed. "Oh, but maybe you'd prefer *café crème*? I will call the waiter again."

"No, it's no trouble. Black is fine."

They sat a moment, waiting. Marguerite excused herself when her cell phone rang. While she took the call, Eleni found herself drawn to someone across the square dressed as the grim reaper, complete with a hooded black robe and an obviously plastic sickle, the tip painted red to appear bloodstained. The hooded figure teased a group of school aged girls who shrieked like a flock of birds when he levered the sickle at them as they passed by on the street.

Amused, Eleni was still smiling to herself when the waiter appeared with the coffee, the sound of heavy stoneware cups rattling against matching saucers tugging her from her reverie.

Marguerite uttered a polite good-bye into the phone, then set it down on the table so she could thank the waiter and pay. Her handbag in her lap, she dug for change, shuffling through the contents of her purse. Eleni unzipped her wristlet, willing to pay, but Marguerite refused to let her. In the end, the vampiress paid for the coffee and offered the waiter a tip of a few Euros because he had stood by with practiced patience, and on such a busy night.

Once he was gone, Eleni tore open a thumb-cup of liquid creamer and poured it into her cup while Marguerite watched. The vampiress sipped her coffee and talked about idle things, things in passing, how much the festival had grown over the years. Then she fixed Eleni with a quiet look from over her coffee cup, her red lips hovering just near the chalk white rim.

"So, do you know where Gisele is?" she asked gently. "Are you going to need a ride home?"

Relief poured through her like blessed sunshine. "Could you do that?" Eleni asked. "Drive me home, I mean?"

Marguerite's brows lifted. "Certainly. I wouldn't dream of leaving you stranded."

Eleni's shoulders sagged, and she breathed deeply. "Thank you. Really. I know Gisele will have to go back to the car eventually." She glanced back toward the town square, wary. "But I can't remember where we parked. It was on a little side street, and there was a lot of traffic."

"No worries." Marguerite shook her head. "Though I will say, you should watch yourself with Gisele in the future. She is rarely trustworthy."

"I suppose you would know," Eleni said wistfully. "Julian said she lived with you for a while."

"That much is true. I took her in for several years. She was very young, so I hired a local woman from the village to be a nurse to her. She grew up in my house, although admittedly, there were times it wasn't easy to live with her. She was strong-willed as a girl, so angry at the world." Marguerite shook her head. "But I am sure you likely know that or you wouldn't be sitting here with me."

Eleni looked down into her coffee to escape those knowing eyes.

They finished their coffee, then left the little café, heading toward a side street around the corner from the central square. It wasn't far from the café or the restaurant where Eleni had dined with Julian, but it was perceptibly darker. Cars lined the streets, which were far quieter and less traveled than the ones at the opposite side of the square.

Even so, there were revelers—late arrivals parked out here, people that grouped together, traveling in packs from their cars to the festivities in the square.

"What you must understand about Gisele," Marguerite told her confidentially, "is that she lived with me as a sort of trainee. I was expected to show her how to be a proper lady, and yet, she was told she would be a servant. I tried to tell Julian that you can't have it both ways. There were places we could send her so that she would be brought up properly, but he was hesitant to send her. He felt sorry for her, I think. She had no family, no one but us to care for her." They reached Marguerite's car, and the vampiress turned and faced her on the sidewalk.

"Julian paid for Gisele's boarding school, and when she was sixteen, he took her into his household as a servant. We both knew she wasn't prepared, but she was a smart girl, charming when she wanted to be, and Julian figured she would catch on. I feared he would cross the line and make her some...bastard lover. But he surprised me. I realized at Christmas the following year, his feelings were more like a father to a daughter—not romantic. Still, I could see the admiration in her eyes, and I warned him she was at an impressionable age, and he would only complicate things for himself and her if he didn't place her under the care of the council." She shook her head. "He feared the council would dismiss her, and likely they would have...for just reasons."

"What did he do?" Eleni asked quietly.

"He sent Gisele to live with me, part time, and without consulting him, I had a life coach come in from Paris, a vampiress with much experience. It was not a success. I knew Julian wanted her to have a "motherly" influence in her life, you see. But Gisele turned against me completely. She has a vicious side once she feels you have wronged her. Mark my word on that. Julian has a soft spot for her, one that I don't entirely understand, but an important thing to know."

She turned with her keys in hand and unlocked the passenger side door, which automatically unlocked all the other doors in the car.

An undercurrent of tension hung in the air. Eleni noticed Marguerite's shrewd tone and ventured carefully, "Something happened between you and her?"

"That depends on who you ask," Marguerite said as she walked around the car to the driver's side door. "As I was saying, the trouble…it depends on who you ask. But I will tell you Gisele is unquestionably ambitious. It is only my opinion, of course, but I believe Julian should have severed the bloodline when her mother left the servitude. Gisele never should have been brought into our homes. It takes years, generations, to build loyalty and trust. We place our lives in the hands our servants, when you think about it. Julian, he…how do you say?" Her eyes clouded thoughtfully, then cleared. "With Gisele, he created a monster. Gisele covets immortality too much, and doesn't have the discipline of a proper servant."

"You think she's dangerous?"

"That depends on what you consider to be dangerous," Marguerite said without guile. "Not long after Gisele came of age, she presented herself to me as a lover. She said she would do anything I desired of her. But, in return, she wanted me to make her a vampire. If she could not be immortal, she would rather I kill her then and there. That was when I packed her clothes and sent her to Julian." Her eyes glittered dangerously, her lips thinned in anger. "Honestly, I'm surprised she hasn't tried to seduce him. But who am I to criticize, yes? After all, Gisele is not a demon of my making. In the end, she is Julian's problem.

All I have ever tried to do is keep my cousin from being lost to loneliness and despair."

Marguerite climbed into the car. For a moment, Eleni stared after her, dumbfounded by this new and surprising information. It explained so many things—Gisele's anger when she was asked to serve the household, and her curious dislike of Marguerite. Also, it at least partially explained her argument with Claudette.

Of course, Julian would be furious if he ever found out what Marguerite had told her. He was a private man, and in some ways, what she'd been told changed the entire dynamic of the household. Eleni knew she could no longer look at Gisele as merely an idle threat.

While it disturbed her that Gisele was so driven to seek immortality, it wasn't necessarily a problem she hadn't faced before. Many Acolytes thought the way Gisele did. The only difference was that the uninitiated, foolish women like Gisele had no idea how rare it was to be chosen for such a gift. Being made a vampire was to share an intimate link with one's creator. Most Acolytes never entered a blood bond with their Biter. Overall, maybe one percent was spared a mortal's death—like her sister Anya. Eleni didn't anticipate ever being so lucky. And after her disastrous relationship with Rubio, she had finally come to terms with that.

Marguerite started the engine, and as Eleni climbed into the car, an odd sense of dread trickled through her at the thought of going back to the chateau. The vampiress rummaged around in the center console for a moment and came away with a pair of gradient sunglasses that were a translucent, smoky gray along the lower half of the lenses for driving. She put them on and looked over at Eleni.

"*Voila.* Are we ready to go?" she asked.

Eleni sucked in a deep breath and nodded. A thousand questions churned in her mind as they pulled away from the curb. Although she wasn't too thrilled with what she'd learned tonight, if she hadn't allowed Julian to shove her out of the nest to attend the festival, she might have never known the truth about Gisele's behavior and her past.

They'd gone less than two blocks when the car slowed and Marguerite swore softly, drawing Eleni's attention to the road ahead, the view a bleary sea of gleaming red taillights. The traffic had bottlenecked along a narrow but main artery running through the village, and up ahead a police officer was waving drivers along a perpendicular street, trying to untangle the snag in traffic.

While Marguerite drummed her nail on the steering wheel in impatience, Eleni looked through the window and noticed a bistro less than ten feet away with a wrought iron balcony and chipped plaster front. In the glowing, amber-sconce ambiance of the front window, which was partly covered with sheer lace, a woman with long, curling blond hair sat with her elbow on the candlelit table.

Gisele.

Anxiety trilled up from the core of Eleni's stomach and lodged in her chest as the car inched along, closer to the window and Gisele. Her lips parted slightly as she watched Julian's troubled servant having a very animated discussion with someone—a man. She couldn't get an immediate good look at him, his back was turned to her, but she could see the reddish brown hair and a pale hand clasped around a steaming cup of coffee or tea.

At last, the car began to roll forward, and as Marguerite drove past the window, the man leaned in as if to share something in confidence with Gisele. Eleni caught a glimpse of his face and paled in shock and disbelief. A dart of alarm stabbed her straight in the heart when she realized the man was Liev Sidorov, the vampire who had come to Julian's house to threaten her.

At that same moment, as if somehow Eleni had drawn her gaze with a thought, Gisele glanced out at the street, her eyes skimming absently over the traffic...until they touched on Eleni's face. Gisele registered an instant expression of shock that made the vampire turn his head to see what had alarmed her so.

A shiver passed through Eleni as the woman's dark brown eyes locked with hers in a remote expression of disbelief.

Intense but brief, the connection lasted until the traffic began moving again. Their eyes slid away from each other as the car passed the bistro, but the chill warning that settled in the pit of Eleni's stomach didn't go away even as she faced forward in time to watch Marguerite navigate them through the slow flowing traffic to freedom.

She knew in her heart the real battle with Gisele had just begun.

Chapter Fifteen

Marguerite dropped her off in front of the chateau shortly after midnight, and waited with the car running to see her go into the house before driving off. Eleni watched through the slim window by the door as Marguerite's car turned around in the driveway and left.

Eleni locked the door, set the code for the alarm, then turned and began to strip off her pea coat. Her worry over the vampire and Gisele meeting in the square had secretly grown into anger on the on the ride home. She knew a threat when it presented itself to her, and she couldn't think of another damn reason one of Rubio's men would contact a member of Julian's household unless it meant trouble for her.

She hung her coat in the closet and headed across the foyer to the stairs. If Julian wanted to see her, he could seek her out. Tired and irritable, she went up to her room, wondering what Rubio hoped to get out of it by sending people to track her down in France. Revenge?

Did he think loss of her status wasn't enough? The threat to her bloodline? Why come after her now? She hadn't concerned herself with him since…she couldn't remember exactly when, but certainly not since she'd received treatment for her Biter's Addiction. She just couldn't understand it.

He had put her through hell, and cutting her ties with him was the best thing that could ever have happened to her, even if the separation had started out as involuntary. Now she had this possible connection with Gisele to worry about. If her suspicions were right, the young woman was a perfect target for Rubio's lies—angry at the world, not well versed in the rules of vampire society, and hungry for someone to make her immortal—something Rubio had no problems promising if it were for his own gain.

Of course, Gisele would have no way of knowing that a bastard like Zander Rubio promised the blood bond time and again to women, never with any intention of making them immortal. He had made the very same promise to her, and led her down a destructive path that had nearly cost her everything, including her life.

"Where is Gisele?" Julian asked from the doorway. She hadn't realized he'd followed her upstairs.

"You'll have to ask her," she said stiffly as she sat on the edge of the bed to pull off her boots. "She abandoned me by the car the minute we arrived in the village."

He stared into her eyes, studying them. "You're serious. How did you get home?"

"Marguerite drove me. We ran into each other in the Square."

"How convenient," he said, and something about his tone struck her as suspicious and insulting.

"Yes, it was. Very convenient, and I'm grateful for that." Her voice simmered with quiet intensity. She wondered vaguely if he had been waiting up for her. If so, she wasn't in the mood for his jealousy. "I would have called the chateau and asked you to come and get me, but it occurred to me that I don't know the phone number here. I don't even have your cell number, Julian, but then what do I need that for when your trusty servant knows the number, right?"

"There is no reason for you to be angry with me," he said, and whether he intended it or not, his thick accent made it sound like a snarl. "I'll have a talk with Gisele when she gets home."

"And do what? Scold her? Ground her and send her to her room?" She looked at him with doubt as she stood up and began to unweave her hair from the braid. "You do that. You have a talk with her. In the morning, I'll call my sister and have a talk with her."

"Whatever the hell for?" Now, he seemed to get it. Something had happened. Something that involved Gisele serious enough to prompt a desire to go back to San Francisco. She'd thought for a minute she'd have to beat him over the head with it, but in the blink of an eye, he shifted from casual to drop dead serious. "What will that accomplish?"

"I'll be able to see what my options are," she shot back. "If you're going to allow your servant to walk over my back and kick me every chance she gets, I'm going back to the States." Her voice trembled with every word as she turned from him and walked to the dresser. She glanced at him in the big mirror. "I can't stay here. I realize that now. Not as long as Gisele is here. I'm not about to make you choose between us, but she is out to get me and I'm not going to stand for it."

"What the hell are you talking about?" He walked around to the edge of the dresser so she had no choice but to face him. "It's Marguerite—she's been talking, filling your head with nonsense."

"It's not nonsense," Eleni blurted angrily. "I'm smart enough to recognize the difference. Marguerite simply told me what you wouldn't. And don't look at me like that, either, because it's not like she said something I didn't already suspect. She told me about Gisele's ambitions of being immortal, and even if she hadn't, Gisele herself told me you love her—it's no wonder, really, since you harbor her here like a spoilt child. Regardless of how you really feel, she loves you, even if it's superficial. Hell, it could be only in her mind. Whatever the case, I know it's only because she thinks you will turn her—and she sincerely believes you will. Even if she has to manipulate you to do it."

He swore in French, his words harsh with denial. But Eleni wasn't moved, she knew better. There was no denying what she'd seen back in the village.

"Fool yourself all you like, Julian. In Gisele's eyes, I'm the only obstacle standing in the way of what she wants most."

Julian appeared momentarily stunned, as though the idea had never been presented to him. His expression darkened. "Is that how Marguerite offered to help—by making you jealous of one of my housekeepers?"

"Jealous?" She gaped at him. "I'm not jealous. I think Gisele's dangerous. And what is wrong with giving Claudette her due? She is your housekeeper...your only housekeeper. I've never seen Gisele lift a finger, even when you asked her to do something specific. I don't understand why you keep defending her."

"Perhaps for the same reason you keep defending my cousin," he snapped. "It sounds like she offered you more than a ride home. She helped feed you a line of shit." His breathing had quickened, gone shallow. Eyes sly, his voice rumbled low. "I suppose after Marguerite volunteered all this grand information, she offered to help you with your condition, also? Let me know when she invites you to move in."

"What condition would that be, Julian? The Biter's Addiction, or the condition of being constantly threatened by Gisele? Don't you even care to know where she was tonight? Who she was with? I saw her in the village with that same vampire that came here wanting me to sign a contract with my ex-Biter. But I suppose that is perfectly all right, because who would dare hurt poor Gisele's feelings, am I right?"

"You're sure? Gisele was speaking to a vampire?" His face held disbelief.

"I saw her with him when I got into Marguerite's car. They were sitting together at the little bistro with the upstairs balcony."

He shook his head. "Gisele has many friends in the village, human friends. Maybe—"

"Do you honestly think I can't tell the difference? I'm not blind, Julian. It was the same man who came here to the house—and he was most definitely a vampire. And not just any vampire, one with ties to my ex-Biter!"

She took out her earrings one by one and dropped them carelessly onto the dressing table.

"Gisele hasn't been coming home during the day for weeks—maybe a month," she said. "Even Claudette has noticed her absence. I heard them arguing about it in the sunroom, about that and other things. Now there's this, and my probationary hearing is coming up soon. The council could very well call members of your household staff to go on statement about my behavior." Her voice shook with conviction. "Gisele already wants me gone. And if that Liev Sidorov person, or Rubio, were to offer her money, or sponsorship, in exchange for a statement against me, I don't doubt for a minute she would take it. She has no loyalty to me, I doubt she has a loyal bone in her body, and who knows what Rubio and Liev could have promised her?"

He was silent as Eleni's eyes flicked over his face.

"I won't stand by and let my bloodline be ruined by her, Julian."

"Well, I can see you and Marguerite put some thought into this," he said at last.

She frowned at him. "Despite what you think of me, Marguerite is only a friend—the only one I've made since I moved here. Surely, that was your intention when you sent her to pick me up from the airport."

"That was my intention, yes. But I also know my cousin has a preference for beautiful women. She has quite a collection of them. You should visit her sometime. I think you would find it most enlightening. I think you would be amazed. You could see with your own eyes that she doesn't treat her own Acolytes the way she treats you."

"Now who is talking nonsense? Marguerite has never hit on me, or acted inappropriately toward me in any way. It would hurt her to hear you talk about her this way."

He had the good grace to look flustered. It came and went quickly, replaced by an expression of cold fury. "Marguerite is hardly some delicate flower, I can assure you of that. You're not only an Acolyte, Eleni, but a tyros living under the court's supervisions—vulnerable and ripe for the picking. You think she doesn't realize that?"

His words slashed pain over her heart. Eleni's mouth gaped, and a hurt sound tumbled out of her. "Is that how it is, then? You're going to pull status on me?" She'd had enough. "Go ahead and bury your head in the sand. I can't stop you. But I won't put on blinders to comfort you. I didn't come here to be bullied by your staff or to be made prisoner inside this house."

Fury was evident in the taut lines of his face. "You are testing my patience."

"How often has Gisele heard you say those words?" *Likely, never.*

Disgusted, she turned away from him and stormed off to the bathroom to wash her face. Leave him there to stew in his jealousy—it served him right. But she had apparently struck a nerve in him, because by the time she'd reached the bathroom door, Julian had caught up with her. He moved in front of her in a blur of motion. His hand caught her arms, his strong body blocking her path.

"I don't wish to fight with you like this," he grated. "I told you I feel a responsibility to give Gisele a decent life. I won't be made to feel guilty for my actions. While I'd be overjoyed to see her end up in a suitable love match, she is not of any noble bloodline and I'm not so charitable that I'd risk the name of my ancestors to marry her myself. I've already told you before that I do not love her. And even if I did feel for her in that way, I don't have the authority to make her an Acolyte."

"Perhaps you should explain that to her."

The sound of a car pulling into the gravel drive silenced them both. Muttering a curse under his breath, Julian went to one of the bedroom windows overlooking the front yard. Eleni stood back with her arms crossed.

"Looks like Gisele decided to cut her date short. I figured she would when she saw me in Marguerite's car." She flicked back her hair. "I wonder what excuse she'll give you for dumping me off in town. Surely, she's thought up one by now."

"Enough," he snapped at her. For a long minute, he stood looking out over the drive, at the car and Gisele, observing her arrival. Finally, he dropped the curtain and started toward the bedroom door. "Stay in here," he ordered.

Eleni didn't argue. There was no time. He left the room, slamming the door behind him.

She flinched at the loud bang that kicked her heart into an anxious gallop. The tension in the air was unbearable even after he had gone, leaving her no choice but to pace the room to cope with it. She had no idea what he was about to do, but she knew that after tonight was over, whether for better or for worse, the household dynamics wouldn't be the same.

Giselle probably had an idea of the storm she was walking into and had probably come up with a thousand passable excuses. The woman was a skilled liar, and Eleni worried about that because Julian had an obvious soft spot for her. When she'd agreed to take up residence with a mal vampire, for what that degrading title was worth, she'd never imagined she'd have to defend her own honor.

Defiance surged in her at the thought of sitting idly by to have her future determined for her. Tired of playing by the rules and getting nowhere, she ignored Julian's order and left her room. She left the door slightly open and padded her way down the hall toward the stairs.

She had no real plan in mind except to hear what he said to Gisele. She wanted to hear his judgment passed down in its original context, and if he sided with his servant, she had already made up her mind that their relationship was over. The thought of losing him lashed pain across her heart—she never could have guessed how attached to him she'd become in such a short amount of time. But she had been through enough in her life with Rubio. She only wanted peace, not to have to put herself on guard at every turn. It simply wasn't worth it.

Before she ever made it to the landing, Eleni heard Julian's voice booming from downstairs, and a woman sobbing. The wracking cries were broken only by shrill pleading in French. The violent notes of her voice rose up to clutch at her heart—Gisele. Julian had apparently caught her right as she had entered the house and launched into her.

Eleni stopped in her tracks and leaned her back against the wall as the wails rose in pitch, and Julian's angry words echoed through the foyer and shivered through walls.

"You have betrayed my trust to another vampire," he snapped at her. "You abandoned my protégé on the streets for hours and met privately with a transient vampire, putting my entire household at risk—"

"No, no…It's not true—"

"Do you call me a liar in my own house?" he roared at her. "There are witnesses!"

"Don't do this, Julian… Please, don't kick me out. I love you too much!" Gisele's sobs were pitiful, desperate, but Julian had already determined the truth for himself.

Eleni couldn't stand it. She'd heard enough. She closed her eyes and covered her ears with the palms of her hands to escape the cries and the shouting. She turned on her heel and headed back to her room. Memories of Rubio ripping her apart in front of the other Acolytes haunted her. The loathing she'd seen in his eyes, and in the eyes of the women she had lived with. She wouldn't wish that on anyone.

Gisele's pleas sounded so familiar and haunting, once she rounded the corner and faced the door to her bedroom at the end of the hallway, she broke into a jog.

Eleni dashed into her room and shut the door, then turned away from it, her hand covering her mouth. She thought about locking herself in, but she could just imagine Julian's reaction if he came back upstairs and found himself locked out.

Instead, she left the door unlocked and went to her closet, spurred by fear, by ghosts of the past. She took down a suitcase from the overhead shelf and carried it to the bed. There, she flopped it down on the end of the mattress, throwing open the latches so the case lay flat.

She went back to the closet and began dragging clothes off the racks, taking them down, hangers and all, and carrying them to the bed to dump in the suitcase. She told herself that Anya would understand. She would have to. There was no other option. Surely, her sister would not turn her away. A vague plan to take one of the cars in the garage and drive to Paris formed in her mind. She had no idea what she would do once she made it to Paris, or back to the States, but it would be better than this, better than living in fear.

The crunch of tires in the driveway followed by a horn blaring drew her attention to the window. She stared. Then she snapped out of that quick moment of empty thought and hurried over to the spot where Julian had stood earlier. Eleni pulled back the curtain, and to her surprise, a black car waited out front with the engine running.

While she watched, Henri got out of the car, his distinctive brown cap covering his head. He walked around to the back door on the passenger side and opened it. Standing beside the car, he stared toward the front door as if waiting.

Eleni heard Gisele and Julian before she saw them. Gisele was shrieking, crying, clinging to Julian as he escorted her out of the house. Henri helped maneuver her into the backseat, struggling with the woman when she would have clung to the open front of Julian's shirt.

Eleni couldn't hear what they said, but the tone carried up to her, and her nerves stretched taut as a wire. Henri finally got Gisele in the car and shut the door, and when he turned, Julian spoke with deliberate, animated gestures. Without a doubt, he was furious.

Henri nodded and went around the car to drive Gisele wherever he had been ordered to take her. Julian stood in the same spot, watching the car roll away down the drive. Only after the taillights had vanished behind the shield of night-dark trees did he turn to head back into the house. Eleni dropped the curtain quickly into place and stepped back from the window, her heart pounding.

Her hand to her throat, she turned and looked around the room at the open suitcase on the bed. Only then did she realize tears were streaming down her face. She went to the bathroom and began gathering her toiletries for her trip. She'd just made it back to the suitcase on the bed when the door flung open to her room. Eleni flinched back. Julian stood there, his eyes gone black with anger.

"I will not have discord in my house." He growled the words as he entered her room and slammed the door. Eleni jumped.

"Julian," she whispered. "What have you done?"

"I did what you wanted me to do, am I wrong?" he asked bitterly. "I have dealt with her, and now there is only you. I also sent a message to my beloved cousin that you're not available, and she is not to seek out your affections. Be aware, Eleni," he snarled under his breath, "I do not share my protégés, ever. Not with Marguerite. Not with anyone. It will serve you well to remember that."

Her mouth opened in shock. Before she had a chance to defend Marguerite as a friend and nothing more, Julian's gaze fell on the suitcase. His mouth twisted, and in two long strides, he crossed the room and shoved the heavy suitcase, clothes and all, off the bed as though it weighed nothing. Then in a rapid blur of movement, he turned and pulled her roughly into his arms.

"You are mine, do you understand?" he snarled, showing a flash of fangs. "You belong here with me."

Chapter Sixteen

Julian's mouth came down on hers in a demanding kiss that sent sparks skittering through her veins. Eleni drew in a sharp breath when he dragged her up against his body and held her close, his hands firm and caressing along her back. She sensed his anger and some other emotion coursing through him, something desperate that held him on edge. Bracing herself against him, she eased her arms up and around his neck.

He backed her up to the bed, and when the backs of her knees touched the edge of the mattress, he eased her down and climbed over her, careful to keep his weight off of her.

He undressed her, skimming back fabric with the flick of a wrist, the smoothing glide of a palm. Following his lead, aware of his intention to make love to her, she helped him unbutton his trousers. When he wore nothing but his crisp white shirt, she parted her thighs, allowing Julian to settle himself there.

His silvery eyes locked onto hers with heated promise. Lowering his head, he gave precious attention to her erect nipples, kissing a hot trail from one taut bud to the other. Sighing softly, Eleni ran her hands through his long black hair, welcoming his body as he rose over her, levering his erection against her wet entrance. Tracing her hands along his shoulders, she smoothed her hand beneath the shirt he wore to hide his scars from her, felt the evidence of old pain, and kissed his collarbone in a silent question. Julian wouldn't allow her to take his shirt off.

She knew the scars were there, a part of him. Despite their earlier argument, and the fact the evening had turned into an awful mess that neither of them had planned, he didn't have to hide his flaws from her. She could never lay judgment against him, especially over something so superficial, something that happened completely out of his control.

Though the scars didn't bother her in the slightest, she could imagine what they must represent to him as an immortal being. She wasn't about to make light of self-consciousness. It would be an insult, and Julian didn't deserve that.

"You don't have to hide from me," she whispered instead, kissing his throat, his chin. "We both have our scars, Julian. The only difference is mine aren't visible."

It was the truth.

Julian stilled and looked down at her, his eyes clouded with some dark emotion. Eleni thought for a moment that she had lost him, killed the moment. But a second later, the tension drained from his body. His pale eyes watched her face as he allowed her to remove his shirt.

They made love—each caress, each stroke slow and passionate, their bodies entwined, clinging to one another as if by doing so they clutched at life itself.

When at last they were both sated, she noticed Julian's fangs hadn't retracted. She wondered when he'd last fed. Of course, she had not asked him. Realizing that she had forgotten made her blush. Even if she had been so wrapped up in her problems with Gisele she could barely think straight, it was still her duty to see that he had the blood he needed to survive.

He hadn't asked because it wouldn't be gentlemanly to do so. She also realized he would not bite her without permission.

She marveled at this sudden revelation. Rubio had never asked her permission, he'd merely fed from her when it had suited him. And she had been happy to give…to the detriment of her own health.

Julian's unspoken gesture of respect touched her to her soul. She stroked her hand across his jaw, loving him with her eyes while she drew aside the curtain of her hair. When he looked at her in question, she settled back in the pillows, offering her throat to him.

"Are you sure?" he asked, his voice remarkably sensual and deep.

"My blood is yours alone."

That contemplative look was on his face again. She wished she knew what it meant.

Tenderness lingered in his touch as he stroked his thumb over her lips before he leaned forward and pressed his mouth to her throat. Eleni tensed, waiting, expecting the sharp pinch of fangs even as his lips caressed the curve of her shoulder, his tongue stroking over her wet skin.

Finally, his teeth pierced her skin, the fiery pain instantly dissolving into a delicious throb of pleasure.

Minutes later, Eleni turned onto her side to try to go to sleep. Now she was not so much upset, but hurt still lingered. Not that she expected Julian to understand. To her surprise, almost as soon as she thought it, Julian rolled over closer and pulled her into his arms. For a long time, they lay there idly without speaking while Julian caressed her hip.

Even after an hour of lying there, she struggled to sleep. Instead, she listened to the hiss of the fireplace and reminded herself why she shouldn't fall in love with Julian. After Rubio, she could ill afford those emotions again, but a part of her warned that where Julian was concerned, it was already too late.

Julian lay on his back staring at the ceiling in the premiere suite, Eleni snuggled close to his side. For as long as he had lived in this house—well over three hundred years—he had never slept in this room.

But after making love to Eleni twice and feeling her body respond to him, he didn't dare break the quiet, contented mood that followed. After the upheaval that had landed on his doorstep unexpectedly earlier in the night, he deserved this rare moment of peace. Still, he couldn't stop thinking about his argument with Eleni.

Now that the dust had settled, he analyzed the fear that had churned inside him, the hopelessness that had gripped his heart and clenched it in an iron fist, when he had realized Eleni planned to leave him.

Julian remembered the time he had been kicked in the chest by a horse at the age of twelve. He had been warned away from the stables and that beautiful, yet disagreeable stallion many times by his older brothers, but he wouldn't listen. He craved nothing more than to touch, soothe, and attempt to tame. The horse would have none of it, naturally. He believed it had tolerated him the way one must sometimes weather an annoying fly. Then, one day he'd snuck into the stallion's stall and the horse had had enough. He'd made a mistake in thinking the horse had grown accustomed to him, and the next thing he knew, the animal had kicked him so hard, if he had been human, it would have killed him.

He'd admitted to his father later that in the seconds before the kick, he had known it was coming. Even now, he vividly remembered that split second of anticipation, a horrible awareness that he stood in the path of danger and destruction, and there not being even a scattered few seconds of time to brace for impact.

He'd felt that feeling again when he'd looked in Eleni's eyes and realized she was serious about leaving him. Inside, he had unraveled a little. He couldn't imagine going back to a life empty of her. Even now, he didn't know how it had come to this, but there it was. He was afraid of losing her.

So many things she'd said hurt him because they were regrettably true. For years, he had allowed Gisele to get by with more than he should have because he felt sorry for her. Marguerite had warned him about doing so for years, and lately, Claudette had come to him with complaints that Gisele was lazy and disagreeable. The accusations and warnings had always been easy to brush aside...at least until they put him at risk of losing his protégé.

He didn't always understand his need to save Gisele, but that time was now over. He vowed he would not lose Eleni over Gisele's foolishness.

Julian looked at the window. He could feel the dawn approaching. If he planned to sleep in this room, he would have to prepare it.

Eleni never stirred when he left her side. Quietly, he padded from window to window, closing the shutters to block out the sun. It was a quick chore, and within minutes, he was about to go back to bed, back to Eleni, when he thought about the bedroom door.

He hesitated, but after carefully considering it, he walked over to the door and locked it.

Julian returned to bed after that. He eased down next to Eleni and pressed a kiss to the top of her head. She smelled like the rose bath soap she always used. It was a scent he could have breathed in forever. There were so many things about her that pleased him. Before tonight, he had thought himself incapable of feeling after the fire, incapable of caring, but she had proved him wrong. Just the thought of losing her was enough to fill him with unbearable anguish.

Chapter Seventeen

In the days that followed Gisele's removal from the house, Eleni began to unwind. It hadn't been easy at first. Gisele made several attempts to contact Julian for various reasons, but he wouldn't allow her back into the house, not even to get her clothes and personal items.

While he did everything he could to dissuade the woman, at the end, he called a meeting with both Henri and Claudette, and informed them both they were to call the police if Gisele showed up unannounced on the property.

On the Sunday following Gisele's expulsion from the chateau, Marguerite arrived looking tired and weary. She had two of her protégés with her, nearly identical golden brunettes who she introduced to Eleni as Oksana and Caprice. Both women were tall and thin as wisps. They neither smiled nor spoke. They had come to help Marguerite, who had brought boxes to collect the rest of Gisele's things.

"How is she doing?" Eleni had asked Marguerite in passing, in those few moments when someone wasn't hovering nearby so she could broach the subject. A box in her arms, Marguerite had shaken her head, her dark eyes full of concern. "She...does not cry as often as she did, but..." She took a deep breath and exhaled softly. "She is not very well, Eleni. Gisele has never viewed herself as anything less than an Acolyte. The truth...it's hard for her to accept. She blames all of us, you know?"

Eleni understood. She knew what it was like to want something you couldn't have, but with time, she would heal. For a while, Eleni had believed she would never bounce back from Rubio's rejection of her. She'd believed that she would wither away in her grief. But now...look at how everything had changed in her life, evolved. She wouldn't trade two seconds with Julian for a lifetime with Zander Rubio.

After Marguerite and her protégés had left, Eleni stood in Gisele's room, empty now, save for a bed, an armoire, and a dresser with a large mirror similar to the one in Eleni's room upstairs. There was also a few throw pillows and magazines, and a framed poster of Van Gogh's *Starry Night*—things that the vampiress had not deemed important enough to take.

Sitting on the edge of the bed, she picked up a magazine and thumbed through it. Images of waif thin, haunted models populated the pages—nothing exceptional, or otherwise out of the ordinary.

She flipped to the cover of the book and read the splash of words across the glossy paper. *Seduce Him with A Glance, and Make Him Love the Real You.* A chill prickled over her skin. She reached out and spread the magazines across the bed like a fan and checked the covers for dates. Gisele had made sporadic purchases. There were sometimes gaps of many months between the issues. But most of the issues had articles about seduction. She sighed, wondering if she was misinterpreting things. Looking too deep for clues that weren't there.

The magazines depressed her rather than made her angry. Gisele obviously had illusions about what it meant to be an Acolyte, some glamorous idea of exclusive privilege, yet unaware of the necessary sacrifices expected of the women who attained it.

Sadly, it was not a new concept among the serving class. Rubio had once had similar problems within his household. Eleni recognized the same stars in Gisele's eyes that had been in Daphne's. Rubio had not been nearly as understanding as Julian. Not only had he cut her from his staff without a second thought, he'd delivered her to the vampire council, along with a petition to sever her family line from service.

"What are you thinking about to put such a frown on your face?" Julian asked her from the doorway. He came into the room, looked around, and sighed. "This is hardly a place to inspire happiness, no?"

She put the magazine down beside the others and slid them into a stack. "I know. I hate that it had to be this way, especially when there are so many things that Gisele and I have in common."

"Is that so?" Julian sounded surprised.

Eleni shrugged. "We grew up not knowing our fathers, and lost our mothers at a young age, and...well, just a lot of similar things." Frowning, she stood up from the bed and went to Gisele's armoire. It was empty. Flicking a glance at Julian, she said quietly, "Gisele was certainly enamored with you, and that's something else we share." She shook her head and turned to face him. "I think it would've been easier for her if she understood that not every Acolyte is made a vampire, and not everyone enters the blood bond."

"I'm sure she must know. I would imagine Marguerite explained it to her as a child." Julian came over to her, put his arm around her waist, and led her from the room. He shut the door, then tucked her arm through his and led her along the hallway. "It doesn't mean Gisele accepted what she was told. Consider the number of Acolytes who refuse to accept it. You can't separate them from their disillusionment. It's a necessary truth that vampires count on to survive: everyone wants to enter the blood bond."

She looked up at him through her lashes. "I wouldn't say that's necessarily true."

Beside her, Julian flinched. He turned to her with bafflement glittering in his eyes. "Are you telling me you wouldn't wish to enter the blood bond?"

Frowning, she hesitated. "Immortality's the prize carrot dangled in front of our noses. That's all I'm saying."

His brows went up. "Should we go back to lurking in the shadows and attacking people in order to survive?"

"Of course not."

"I can't imagine what you think we should do then." There was an edge to his voice. "If not for the blood bond, vampires would have a hard time finding blood donors—and lovers."

She felt suddenly tired, as if she had run too far and too long in an endless race. She sighed and gentled her voice. "You're right. Who doesn't want immortality, Julian? I would be honored to spend eternity with you." She stroked her hand over his arm. "Still, you're missing my point. People like Gisele assume all protégés will eventually be turned." She shook her head. "I feel sorry for her—I wish she could know the truth. My mother was favored. She was adored until the day she died, but no one spoke for her." Eleni choked back the rise in her throat and said quietly, "She would have made a loving, devoted vampiress."

Calm and serious, he picked up her hand and traced his thumb in a caress across her wrist. "And this makes you worry about your own mortality?"

"It used to," she admitted. "But if living with Rubio made me realize anything, it's that I would much rather face death than live an eternity with someone who doesn't love me."

Knowing what she knew now, she cringed whenever she thought about what kind of life entering the blood bond with Rubio would've afforded her. He was cruel, devious, and heartless. It had been difficult enough living with his half-truths and infidelities. In the long run, sharing their thoughts and feelings in a psychic connection would have turned the gift of immortality into a punishment she didn't want or need.

"What about your sister, Anya?" Julian asked. "She is blood bound to Dominic. She will outlive you. That doesn't bother you?"

She started to say no, but stopped herself and thought carefully. "I'm sure when that time comes, it will be harder for Anya to deal with than it will be for me. But, then again, Anya was always the strong one, the smart one. And Dominic was sure about what he was doing. Even then, everyone knew he loved my sister. Please…" She rubbed her hand over her forehead. The conversation was making her tense and giving her a headache. "Can't we talk about something else?"

He turned her to him and wrapped her in his arms. "We both need a break, don't you think? I tell you what. You go upstairs and get dressed. I'll meet you at the door in twenty minutes, and we'll take a drive into the village. What do you say?"

Her heart wasn't really in it, but he was right. It would do them both some good to get out of the house for a while.

"Okay." She nodded. "Sounds good to me."

* * *

Julian took her out to dinner at Chez Gerard, the same place he had taken her on their first outing together. It was comfortable and less crowded than it had been right before the festival. Eleni ate soup and salad, and a slice of walnut cake, and afterwards, Julian surprised her with an invitation to a midnight gala featuring the work of several local artists.

"The theme is fitting," he told her as they walked to the gallery, which was at the far end of the square near the clock tower. "It is about spring being a time of growth and new beginnings."

Eleni liked the concept of new beginnings and hoped she could count this unexpected treat as a good omen for the future. She was feeling optimistic about it when they entered the building and the tide of joyful, excited energy washed over her.

Tightening her arm around Julian's, she leaned closer to him and whispered, "This looks wonderful!"

This seemed to please Julian very much. As they crossed the entryway to approach a small gathering who was chatting and sipping champagne, a hostess with short, ink black hair came forward to check Julian's invitation and greet them.

She stared at the card. "Sévigné…" Her eyes flicked up to his face in surprise.

Julian frowned down at her. "Is there a problem?"

"Not at all! I'm just so surprised, I—" the woman protested, laying the hand with the card over her heart. "Forgive me. I'm Josette Manon." She clasped Julian's briefly in hers. "I handle the funding for the gallery. I'm honored you have decided to join us, Monsieur Sévigné. Your generous donations over the years have meant so much to us."

The woman insisted on introducing Julian to the rest of the staff on hand, as well as several of the artists. Eleni found it all very amusing, the number of people who had heard of Julian, but had never seen nor met him until tonight. They clung to him, walked him around making introductions and pointing out paintings, showing him remodels and innovations to the gallery and studio that his donations had paid for. Eleni beamed with pride, watching him. Here, he could not hide the way he did at the chateau, and yet, Julian didn't appear at all out of his element.

The contact was good for him, and Eleni didn't try to interfere. She wandered around the gallery, chatting with a patron now and again, but mostly moving from room to room to look at the paintings.

Julian finally met up with her as she was standing in front of a series of photographs depicting traditional courtyard gardens, some in full color, and others in black and white. She loved the magical, secluded look of them.

"I'm sorry I was away for so long," Julian apologized as here captured her arm.

"They're curious about you," Eleni teased. She loved the way his eyes were shining, alive with quiet excitement. "Not that I can blame them."

"So it seems. Are you ready to go?"

She looked around. People were leaving, chatting at the door while preparing to go out. A man with a neatly trimmed beard and tan trousers was picking up champagne glasses and setting them onto a tray. "It looks like they're shutting down for the night. There was talk of an after-party. You might get swept away by the crowds again."

"Wicked girl," he said roughly. "I'm ready to go home."

Eleni grinned. "So am I."

Chapter Eighteen

The ride home was quiet and comfortable, almost restful, after visiting the gallery. Eleni enjoyed the night view while Julian drove them back to the chateau. Through her window, the vineyard looked so different now than when she'd first arrived a little over three months ago. It was hard not to notice with the snow was gone, and the leaves breaking out on the vines.

Eleni yawned on her way in through the door when they reached the chateau around a quarter to three. The house had settled for the evening it seemed. The lights were off inside and out, and while the smell of chicken soup permeated the downstairs, the door to the kitchen was closed and there was no sign of Claudette.

"It's late. There's no need to disturb her," Julian said as he stripped off his coat and hung it in the front closet. "If you don't mind, there's a bottle of bloodwine in my office. I'm going to grab a drink before bed. I will join you upstairs in a few minutes, okay?"

Eleni nodded and started away, but Julian grabbed her before she got out of arm's reach and tugged her into an embrace and kissed her quickly on the mouth. "Am I going to find you asleep when I get up there?"

"You just might," she warned, which made him laugh—and kiss her again.

"Ah, all right." He swatted her on the behind. "Go on, then. I'll meet you in bed."

"I'll try not to steal all the covers before you get there," she teased, kissing him on the end of the nose before he finally let her go.

A smile lingered on Eleni's lips as she started up the stairs. Mid-flight, she paused long enough to remove her shoes then padded the rest of the way to her room in her stocking feet, thoughts of Julian and the gallery foremost in her mind. It had been a very long time since she'd had such a good time out on a date.

She flicked on the light, and on her way into the room, tossed her shoes and handbag onto the little chair just inside the doorway. Tired, and ready for a shower, her jewelry was the next to go. She moved around to the dressing table and removed her hairpins and her earrings, dropping them all into one of the little drawers directly under the large, chevron shaped mirror.

Humming to herself, she paused to light a few scented candles, and had just reached into a drawer for a set of pajamas to take with her to the bathroom when out of her peripheral vision she glimpsed movement.

Eleni darted her eyes to the mirror and jumped in startled surprise at the sight of her closet door swinging wide open. A woman with golden blonde hair rushed from the shadows. Eleni spun around right as Gisele lunged at her with a large knife held high. A scream caught in her throat, shrill and rippling.

"You bitch! I hate you! *I hate you!*" Gisele attacked like a berserker. Slashing wildly, she looked like a madwoman with her hair flying around her tear-stained face. Eleni backed away, mouth agape, and lifted her hand to guard her face and felt the white hot sting as the blade sliced across her palm. Her gasp transformed into a shocked cry of pain. Gisele caught her again on the shoulder, and left her forearm in the same strike. A howl of agony broke from Eleni's lips. Fearing for her life, she began to swing blindly, fighting back, sweeping things off the dresser at her attacker—but Gisele wasn't stopping.

They kicked and struggled, toppling the bedside lamp and pulling down the ornamental drapes hanging near the head of the bed. Eleni managed to wrench the knife from Gisele's fingers, but then she stumbled back, her foot tangled in the fallen drapes. The knife spun away, under the bed and out of reach. Gisele shrieked at her in rage and pounced on her, beating her with fists, grabbing her hair and yanking with brutal fierceness. Eleni had a hand braced tight against Gisele's throat, and with her other hand she reached up and slammed the woman on the nose with the heel of her hand. She felt a crunch and blood flowed, but Gisele was deterred for barely a second.

"You can't have him. I won't let you. We were happy before you came! He loves me, I know he loves me—Julian is mine!" Gisele continued to rage as she punched and clawed as Eleni did her best to block the blows and still fight back. Briefly, Gisele ceased, but it was only to reach for something near the bedside table which had upended, and laid half on Eleni's hair. Then Gisele brought her hand back, and raised it up like a fist. Tucked in the palm was something smooth looking and shiny black.

Gisele brought the stone panther statue down on Eleni's head in quick, fierce blows. Eleni felt the first strike through a veil of pain and blunt shock. By the third blow, she went limp.

Her breathing quick and irregular, Gisele scrambled back and sat on her haunches, looking at the Acolyte unconscious on the floor. Her nerves were shot. She looked down at the stone statue in her palm and noticed the way her hand was trembling. The statue tumbled from her fingers and landed with a heavy thud on the floor. She wiped the blood from her hand onto the carpet, as giddy joy rose up from the pit of her stomach when she realized that she had actually done it. She'd taken care of the competition.

For a long minute, Gisele sat beside the bed, trying to center herself. She was cold and shaking all over, her rage spent. Rage that had boiled inside her from the moment

Julian told her he planned to allow the Acolyte whore to live in their house. Now she was numb and didn't know what to do. She had planned to seduce Julian. That was the whole idea. To be his lover, to live forever—to *live*—something her mother had barely had the chance to do.

She glanced over at Eleni's body lying supine. A trickle of fear began to course through her. There would be no way to hide what she had done to her, or to Claudette. Julian wouldn't be happy with her. She hadn't thought that far ahead. It hadn't been her intention to hurt Claudette, but the woman had threatened to call the police. In the thick of it all, she couldn't remember what she'd been thinking, or what Liev had told her...other than to be smart and have patience. He'd told her she wouldn't have to do anything, that if she could only see the woman doing something...inappropriate, or dangerous, she wouldn't have to deal with her anymore.

But Liev was wrong. Julian would never let the council take Eleni. She looked at the blood flowing from Eleni's wounds. Defensive wounds. Now what to do?

Being smart meant leaving no witnesses. And still, she wanted immortality. Julian. Tears streamed down her face as her world came crashing down around her. She was a murderer, a victim of her own jealousy. But all of it was Eleni's fault. If only Julian had taken one look at her and turned her away. She leaned her head against the bed to think, and for a moment, she was mesmerized by the candles flickering on Eleni's dressing table.

* * *

Julian poured a second glass of bloodwine and carried it with him to the elevator to take him up to his room. Tonight at the gallery had taught him a valuable lesson. *I'm getting old,* he thought with dry amusement.

All the way home, he'd felt contemplative and drained, and wondered what Eleni would think of him if he pulled over and asked her to drive the rest of the way back to the house. He wasn't unfit or out of shape, but being led around the social arena for the night was enough to leave him reeling and in need of blood. If his brothers, Charles and Yves, had been around to witness this, they would have fallen back in the apples laughing over this weakness, he just knew it.

He climbed into the elevator with fond memories of his long deceased brothers. How he missed them. He blew out a breath, his thoughts shifting to Eleni and the people he'd met at the gallery. It was good to feel needed, accepted, despite his scars. And yet, he didn't want Eleni to see how weary he was. Not that he thought for a minute she would turn away from him or chide him for needing rest, but because, to his shame, he wanted to impress her.

He loosened his tie before opening the grate and stepping off the elevator on to the second floor. Taking a sip of his drink, he sauntered to the bedroom, ready to hit the bed and settle in with Eleni. He'd prepared himself for her playful teasing, he'd spent more time downstairs than he'd expected, but when he opened the door to his room, it was dark and cold. Empty. Eleni wasn't there. No fire burned in the hearth.

Instantly, Julian sensed that something was wrong. Claudette was meticulous. Her routine was precise and in clockwork order. She was very particular about it. If Eleni realized the room wasn't ready, she would have prepared it herself, and then checked on Claudette. Had she gone downstairs? Was she still in her room?

Alarmed, Julian left the room with unexplained dread spreading through him with every hard beat of his heart. He had just reached the stairs when he smelled smoke. A shiver passed through, a sense of déjà vu that he didn't want to acknowledge, even as a prickle of cool sweat popped out across his body. Breaking into a jog, he hurried crossed the balcony, his thoughts racing. He shouted for Eleni, his voice booming off the walls in desperation, but no one answered, and at the far end of the Acolyte's corridor, the air grew considerably thick and dusky, and distinctly warmer.

Heart galloping with fear, Julian sprinted through a veil of gray smoke that had collected in the hallways like a ghostly cloud. He rounded the final corner leading to the premiere suite and broke into a sprint. Racing toward Eleni's door at the end of the hallway, he felt a sense of unreality, like he had passed inexplicably from one horrible time into another.

The heat reached out to him from beyond the closed door. On instinct, he grabbed for the door handle and gasped in pain as the metal seared his palm like a hot poker. Backing up a step, he steadied himself, his palm smarting, a pulse beating hard in the burned flesh. He kicked the doors open, and the blast of heat from the room staggered him.

Julian flinched back as he looked into the room, into the inferno of rippling, flowing fire. The sound was deafening, a steady rushing roar that crackled and moaned.

Panic washed over him, a cold wave of fear that swept through him and lodged in his stomach like a ball of ice. For a moment, he was back in the past. In that moment which still came to him in his darkest nightmares. The crackling in the room was so loud it sounded like screaming—hellish cries of anguish and agony.

"It's happening again," he rasped in horror. But, at the same time, awareness rose up in him, the memory of a face. His heart leapt to his throat at the thought of Eleni burning, of her screaming for him to help her. Torment gripped him, and along with it, a new determination. A rush of adrenaline surged through him. The thought of losing her forever sent his fear fleeing into a remote part of himself that clamped down on the notion that he had to find her, save her, even if he destroyed himself.

"Eleni!" he shouted as he dashed into the burning room.

Julian searched frantically, squinting through the orange brightness. His skin was instantly drenched in sweat as he turned a small circle and saw flames dancing on every surface of the room. It had crawled up the curtains, bubbled the wallpaper, and was eating through the carpet like a grass fire. He flinched at the fire licking along the ceiling in rolling waves. It was when he turned to escape the room that he saw her through the ripples of wavering heat. Eleni was lying unconscious on the floor near the bed. His heart gave a frantic leap. He rushed over to her and crouched down through the littered debris—signs of a struggle.

He swept her up into his arms, shocked by the sight of blood and the awareness that she wasn't breathing.

He rushed to the door as the ceiling began to rain fire over them. It burned his back, his arms, but he thought only of sheltering Eleni and escape. He stumbled from the room into the hallway. The flames were lapping over the top of the door, pouring fire and black smoke into the hall. Julian had just regained his footing when he glimpsed dark movement out of his peripheral vision. He glanced to the left, and to his stunned horror, he saw a dark form emerge from Eleni's bathroom into the center of the bedroom.

"Gisele!" Julian gasped her name. He almost didn't recognize her. Her sooty face was swollen, her eyes ringed with darkening bruises. Blood streamed from an obviously broken nose. His gaze zeroed in on the bloodstained pullover sweater, the way the smears of blood looked like a macabre finger painting.

His breath held as their eyes locked. Motionless, she watched him, her gaze flat, the flames turning them a glistening shade of ebony. Sweat, or maybe tears, ran through the smudged soot on her cheeks. She looked haunted, distant, and ghost-like. He opened his mouth to call out to her, when without a word, she opened the door on her left and walked into Eleni's closet, closing the door behind her.

In shock, Julian began to run with Eleni in his arms. Halfway down the hall, Gisele's bloodcurdling screams pierced his heart and shivered through the burning walls of the house. Her cries of helpless agony chased him from the room as flames took root in the hallway, pulling the oxygen from the air and devouring the house from the inside out.

Running on automatic, bent on survival, he made his way down the corridor with Eleni in his arms. At the top of the stairs, he paused to boost her higher against his chest. Her body was so slick with sweat and blood, he very nearly dropped her. His lungs burned, and sweat rolled off of him. The heat was incredible, and it was building up in the house at an alarming rate. Eleni's blood had soaked into his shirt and slicked his hands. Looking down at her, he sobbed. She looked so crushed and helpless. He feared she was already dead.

At the bottom of the stairs, he remembered Claudette. Eying the front door, he cursed under his breath. He was right there by the doorway to the kitchen. It would take but a moment to yell at her if she was there.

He veered to the right, kicking the door open with his foot and holding the door open with his shoulder. "Claudette!"

Copper pots boiled angrily on the stove, the lids bouncing, boiling over in foamy stock. The central island with the chopping block surface had various vegetables sliced, the scent of spices and chicken stock and vegetables was as thick as the humidity in the room, but through it all, Julian could also smell the rich tang of blood. He stepped around the edge of the central island and saw Claudette lying on the kitchen floor. He winced in shock at the sight of her, frozen in death. She was covered in blood—someone had slashed her throat with a large knife from the wooden block on the counter. Her eyes were closed but her tongue bulged, her face fixed in an eternal expression of horror.

The cloying odor of raw blood hung thick in the air. It blended with the kitchen smells, the stench of onions and hot oil, and made his stomach turn. There was nothing to be done for his beloved housekeeper. Her life had bled out of her at Gisele's hand. He couldn't save her, and he feared that if he didn't hurry and get Eleni out of the house, he wouldn't be able to save her, either. The heat of the fire would only intensify as it ate into the ancient wooden walls of the house. It seemed as if every surface radiated heat. The entire chateau was going up like a tinder box. He had to get Eleni out of the house now, or they were going to die.

Stepping over Claudette's lifeless form, Julian nearly slipped in the growing pool of blood. He quickly regained his balance, and went to the door leading out to the garage and flung it open. Heat blasted him in the face like the open door of an oven. He backed away, his mind reeling as down the dark tunnel, the sounds of cracking beams echoed, and drops of fire began to rain down.

Turning on his heel, he dashed out of the kitchen and headed toward the front door. The fire hadn't yet reached the foyer, but above, all along the hallway and the balcony, the fire had spread like a huge, rolling wave.

Flames licked at the ceilings and had spread along the carpet, creating a frame of fire around Saint Vincent's window. Julian felt an odd sense of finality while he stared, as the window began to darken and crack. The panes of glass fractured in places, sending shards of colored glass tumbling from the window. Through it all, Eleni never stirred.

Julian hurried out of the house, carrying Eleni across the driveway to a grassy slope. He had just settled her down, was checking for her pulse when he saw a dark shape coming up the hillside toward the house from the direction of the vineyard.

"Monsieur Julian!" It was Henri. The old man had a walking stick and was making his way up the hillside, heading straight for him.

As the driver neared, Julian could see he had his cell phone in his hand.

"I saw the blaze from the small hill and called for a rescue. The fire brigade is on the way." Panting, Henri eased down onto his knees. He swiped his face with a handkerchief and looked around. "What has happened? Where is Claudette?"

"She's dead, Henri. Gisele killed her and attacked Eleni. She has gone mad." Henri stared at him in shock, then looked up at the house that was now billowing smoke, the upstairs windows pouring out flames.

Julian leaned over Eleni and discovered she wasn't breathing. He dipped his head down to listen for a heartbeat, and at that same moment, the peaked roof over the premiere suite collapsed with a sound like cracking, groaning torment. The onrush of oxygen stirred the blaze into an inferno that began to lick a path along the otherwise untouched roof.

Julian began CPR on Eleni. He tilted her head back, opened her mouth, and puffed air into her lungs, all the while praying he was not too late.

"Come on, *mon amour*. Breathe for me." He completed a series of chest compressions, then paused and listened for breath, a heartbeat. Hearing nothing, he repeated the cycle.

Her lips were blue from lack of oxygen. Julian's mind began to race. He worried about death. Smoke inhalation. Dark purple bruises had begun to form on her forehead. It would take at least fifteen minutes for emergency services to arrive, and by then, Eleni would be dead.

"Work with me, Eleni," Julian murmured as he pulled her limp body into his lap. He was shaking, determined, as he angled her across his lap so he could initiate a blood exchange. Henri hobbled forward on his knees to help him pull her into his lap. The old man couldn't have anticipated what he planned to do.

But Julian had no intention of quibbling over details. He couldn't let her go, his only protégé. Not only had she changed his life, she had given him reason to rise from the ashes of the man who had been scarred by the past. He loved her, and he couldn't bear the idea of facing eternity without her.

His eyes on Henri, he offered him a look of warning, then he sank his fangs into Eleni's neck. The sweetness of her blood sprang hot into his mouth, the iron taste of life, of secret immortality pouring down his throat. Her heartbeat was so weak, he was afraid to take too much.

He let go with a gasp and pulled open his shirt. He quickly slashed a line over his heart, and as the blood flowed, he pulled Eleni to him and laid her head against him, but she was unconscious and he struggled to make her drink.

He swore under his breath and looked up at the horror on Henri's ashen face.

"Call Marguerite," he ordered as he stood and gathered Eleni's limp body into his arms and carried her toward his car, which was still parked in the drive. "Tell her I'm on the way and explain what has happened." He swallowed over the lump of fear that threatened to close his throat. "If I don't turn Eleni soon, she will die."

Marguerite was waiting at the front door when he arrived. The outdoor lights were turned on for him, and as he parked in front of her house, Marguerite and two of her protégés stepped outside to offer him assistance. A small cry of shock escaped Marguerite's lips when he tugged Eleni from the car and boosted her up into his arms.

"Julian... is she breathing?" She held the front door open for him as he shuffled into the house with Eleni's limp body held tight against his chest.

"It's begun, Gita. I've already made an exchange with her, but the addiction... it has made her resistant. You must help me."

Marguerite looked suddenly afraid. Julian carried Eleni across the threshold into her house, ignoring several of Marguerite's protégés who were in the sitting room, looking around in alert fascination as he carried Eleni straight up to the room where he stayed when he visited as a guest. He turned the knob and kicked the door open with his foot, then carried Eleni into the room and placed her in the middle of the large bed. The room was country provincial, spacious and closed off from the rest of the sleeping quarters. Julian chose it now because it had blacked out shutters over the windows and a private bathroom.

"How can I help you, Julian? What must I do?"

"She needs more blood. More than I can give alone. You must help me complete the exchange."

She gaped at him. "Do you know what that could do to her?" He didn't answer her. "Are you sure you want to do this?"

"Do I want to save her life?" he asked incredulously. Frowning, he knew what she meant. "She is clinging by a thread, Marguerite. Now is not the time for analyzing our greater desires. But if you're asking me if I'm certain about entering the blood bond with her then—" He looked down at the woman in his arms. "I cannot bear to lose her."

"Julian, what you ask…there is a reason it isn't done. The results would be unpredictable. She could end up blood bound to us both. If it is my blood that turns her, she may end up bound to me."

"I'm aware of that."

"You could lose her entirely."

"I will lose her entirely if she dies," he snapped. "I would not ask this of you, but I love her, Gita. Do you understand?"

Her eyes flicked over his face. "Damn you, Julian." She licked her lips. "I do not like this. You know what a dual exchange could do to her," she said in a low voice. "I adore Eleni, but what you are asking is dangerous. Not just for her, but for all of us. The bond will connect all of us in some way. The results are not predictable. There is a reason why we are only allowed to turn one bloodmate."

He laughed sharply. "I don't need you to lecture me on the subject, cousin."

"With both our voices in her head, it could drive her to suicide."

"If it comes to that, then you can place all the blame squarely on my shoulders." His eyes glittered with impatience. "I know the risks. Now, will you help me? Or will I be arranging for her burial come morning?"

She pulled a face, baring her fangs in frustration. "You are a bastard, you know that? You always must have your way." She ran a shaking hand across her brow and cursed under her breath. Scrambling to her feet, she hurried to the bedroom door, flinging it open and startling several of her protégés who were waiting in the hallway.

"Yvette," she called one of her most trusted Acolytes to the door. "Heat a pan of water," she told the young woman when she was close. "And have Oksana bring spare towels."

"What's going on?" Julian heard one of the young women ask from the hallway.

"Monsieur Julian's bloodmate is dying," Marguerite said quietly. "Now, do as I say. Fetch those things for me—and be quick!"

She shut the door and returned to bed, where Eleni lay like a broken doll across the ivory sheets. Julian looked up at his cousin in silent gratitude. She was already rolling up her sleeves.

"Thank you," he said in a voice that was both rough and weary. "I know this may well take away your one chance to have a bloodmate."

"There are never any perfect choices, are there?" Marguerite sighed, and sat down on the edge of the bed. "Let us save her, and pray we are not too late."

They worked with Eleni for hours, Julian giving her blood first before passing the duty to Marguerite. They each bled for her several times, and through it all, Eleni remained mostly unresponsive, her breathing raspy and irregular. Weak from blood loss, he sat back in a chair beside the bed and didn't argue when Marguerite went to the door and called down for bottles of blood wine to be delivered to Eleni's room.

They drank in silence, bottle after bottle. It was potent, but not enough. Marguerite excused herself and went to feed. She had offered him the blood of one of her protégés as a restorative, but he declined. It seemed wrong in the face of what they were attempting to do.

Marguerite returned a little while later, sated but obviously tired. He hadn't heard her enter. He sat slumped in the chair with his thumb scraping over the bristles of his five o'clock shadow. The tap of a cup against his shoulder make him glance around. His cousin had brought him a large snifter of blood.

"For your strength," she said quietly.

Julian slipped the glass from her hand and watched as she crossed the room and sat in a chair to wait. Beside one of the narrow windows, she smoked cigarettes and watched the glow of the fire on the horizon. Julian drank the blood and felt better, but tired still. His eyelids felt heavy. He absently watched Marguerite sitting in the window until he dozed off.

Around 4:00AM, Eleni awoke in shrieking sobs, her body gripped in throes of agony. Julian leapt up, severed abruptly from a dream of wandering aimlessly through the vineyard. In an instant, he was beside her on the edge of the bed, holding her down to keep her from hurting herself.

"*Mon Dieu!*" he gasped. The whites of Eleni's eyes had turned the color of a dark garnet. Her skin was clammy, yet blazing hot to the touch.

"It's happening," Marguerite grimaced. "The blood… she's turning." She hurried around to the opposite side of the bed and did her best to hold down Eleni's legs.

Eleni writhed, moaned, and hissed for a five full minutes. Then, she began to convulse. Horrified, Julian cursed, shouted in fear at Marguerite, who had no idea what to do.

"Eleni, everything is all right," Julian told her in his most soothing voice, trying to calm her even as he struggled to keep her on the bed. He couldn't risk her hurting herself. Sweat beaded along his brow while turmoil raged inside him.

You must be all right, mon amour. Because I need you—I can't lose you. How would I live?

Almost as soon as he thought the words, a searing white hot pain erupted across his brain. It nearly toppled him. Clenching his eyes tight, he growled and felt his fangs elongate—a defensive reaction. His head swam, and distantly, he could hear Marguerite's voice asking him if he was okay.

Rising up through the agony—the sharp awareness of hunger. His body was on fire with it, the need so strong it nearly took his breath. A minute passed before Julian realized the hunger was not his. It was Eleni's. Their connection had cemented, and his bloodmate needed to feed.

In a flurry of movement, he ripped open his shirt and pulled Eleni close to him. "You need to feed, Eleni. Do you hear me? The pain you feel…only blood will make it stop." *Blood rushing hot and potent through your veins. Drink, love, drink from me.*

He felt her panic, the uncertainty lingering in her mind like a shadow. Then, instinct took over. Julian flinched in ecstasy as Eleni's fangs pierced his flesh.

She stilled as she drank from him. Slowly, very slowly, her pain ebbed away, but in its place, Julian discovered a well of fear and confusion. He let her drink until he could feel the tugging in his veins warning him to stop. When he at last disengaged her fangs from him and laid her back in the bed, she had grown limp, docile. Her expression had grown even more distant.

The room had fallen abruptly silent, the only sound Julian and Marguerite's ragged breathing. They were both still reeling in shock when Eleni's head turned to the side, her gaze regarding her Biter as if through the mist of a dream. "Julian…"

"I'm here, my love. I'm right here," he croaked raggedly.

Without warning, her eyelids drifted closed. Julian hovered over her a long minute, trembling, shaken. He leaned over her, cradled her to him and kissed her hair, murmuring a jumbled litany of relief against her lips.

Finally, Marguerite tugged him away. "Come. We should let her rest."

Chapter Nineteen

They stepped out into the hallway, where Julian stopped and leaned against the wall. Worry ate at him. He ran his hands through his hair, then stood away from the wall and paced. A minute later, he leaned against the wall again and covered his mouth with his hand. He was so stressed it was almost unbearable.

"Julian, you have to be calm." Marguerite laid a hand on his arm. "She will be okay."

"I don't know," he rasped. "I just don't know." He shook his head. "I feel her confusion." He hesitated before admitting what he had noticed while in the room with Eleni. "She senses your emotions."

Marguerite froze. "Are you sure? I don't feel any different," she said in quiet amazement.

"I will take that as a good sign. Then again, you didn't drink from her directly. Even so, I know for certain we're all connected. I can feel Eleni feeling you," Julian confessed and leaned heavily against the wall. He raked a hand through his hair.

"Madame," someone said from behind them. It was a slender young woman with dark hair. Her brown eyes skimmed warily over Julian.

"What is it, Josephine?"

"There is a man at the front door. He says he works for Master Julian."

"Henri," Julian rasped, and pushed past Marguerite. He walked through the house and found the old man standing in the foyer, crumpling his hat in his hands.

"Monsieur, the police came. I told them you weren't home when the blaze started. They're looking for you, nonetheless. I suspect it is to do with Claudette and Gisele. They said you should contact them as soon as possible. This is the inspector's card."

Julian slipped the contact card from his fingers and laid a hand on the man's shoulder. "Thank you, Henri. I will reward you handsomely for your loyalty once this mess is over."

"I am grateful, *Monsieur*, but that is not all of it. Last night, a vampire came to me at my *gîte*. He was well tailored...tall with reddish hair. He appeared to be from the city. The man asked for you, and then asked if the girl, Eleni, had lived through the blaze. I told him I didn't know."

"Did the man give his name?" Marguerite asked.

"No, Madame. He spoke passable French, but his accent was distinctly Russian."

A flame gleamed in Julian's eyes as he turned to Marguerite. "Liev Sidorov."

"You know who it is?" Her brows lifted.

Julian's eyes narrowed. A muscle ticked in his cheek. "He has come to the house before to speak to Eleni. He's a representative of Zander Rubio, Eleni's former Biter."

"Are you sure? It could have been someone from the council. The fire at the chateau has been in the news."

Julian had already guessed that much. He knew for sure the fire had been reported as far as Paris. Eloise, the housekeeper at his townhouse, had tried to phone him many times. He had waited until Eleni was resting comfortably before he returned her call.

Julian turned to Henri. "Did the vampire say where he was staying?"

"*Non, Monsieur*, but by the cut of his clothes, I don't think he would choose poor accommodations."

Julian thanked his servant, and offered to find a place in the village for him to stay, but Henri had lived in the *gîte* for over thirty years—it was his home. He was determined to remain in the former rental cottage, and Julian had no desire to take that small comfort from him.

The following night, Julian gave his statement to police. The inspector from the village had traced him to his cousin's house. He answered their questions as thoroughly as possible, yet was careful not to go into overly elaborate detail of his whereabouts, since he didn't know what

Henri had already told them. Curiously, they didn't ask him about Eleni. Perhaps they did not realize she had lived at the chateau. Whatever the case, he certainly wasn't going to mention her. She was not in any state to face questioning by the police.

The inspector didn't stop with the one interview. After Julian, they questioned Marguerite, and also, briefly, Marguerite's premiere, Oksana, who sat demurely on the sofa and obviously knew nothing about the fire, or the typical goings-on at the chateau. The inspector lingered a few moments after that, looking around with great interest at both the arrangement of the house and Marguerite's protégé, Antoinette, who had arrived late, and sat like a haughty bronze goddess in one of the leather wingback chairs.

Finally, the inspector gave Julian his card and said he would be in touch if he needed any more information. He didn't seem to think he would.

Once the police were gone, Julian went upstairs to check on Eleni. In the dimly lit room, he walked over to the bed and looked down over his sleeping bloodmate. She had curled on her side with her hands tucked protectively against her body.

Overall, she slept soundly and didn't seem to be in any pain. Julian was glad for that. He brushed her hair back from her forehead and leaned down to drop a tender kiss on the bruise that darkened her forehead near the hairline. On his way out of the room, he grabbed his sport coat off the corner chair.

When he came back downstairs with his keys in his hand, Marguerite looked up from a book she was reading. There were dark shadows under her eyes. She sat straighter and closed the book. "You're going out?"

He couldn't tell her where. Several of her protégés had joined her in the sitting room. They lounged about in front of the television where they could overhear him.

"Keep an eye on, Eleni," he told her. "I'll be back before dawn."

He walked to the front door and let himself outside. For a moment, on the edge of the walkway, he stopped and looked out over the horizon, past the silhouette shape of sprawling walnut trees where an orange glow hung in the sky in the direction of his chateau. It still burned. The police had warned him it would likely burn for days.

His heart clenched as though a vise had gripped it. Losing the house was like losing a first love. It had been his sanctuary for hundreds of years. But even as he stood and gulped in the cool night air, he knew that even if he rebuilt the house, it would never be the same. His life revolved around Eleni now.

He'd just taken the first few steps toward his car when the front door opened behind him. He glanced back, waiting as Marguerite walked toward him, her hands fisted on the gap of a tan cardigan she'd apparently thrown on quickly before stepping outside.

"Where are you going? Surely, not to your chateau?" Her eyes were worried.

"I have to find Liev Sidorov before he leaves the village."

She was silent a moment. "Do you think that's wise?"

"I have to go. I have to find out what her Biter wanted from her and what he had been discussing with Gisele that pushed her to do what she did." If Eleni's Biter wanted to war with him, he was more than willing to accept the challenge.

"Julian, you must be careful." Marguerite lowered her voice. "If anyone were to find out what we have done for Eleni—"

"Unless you plan to tell someone, no one will ever know." His eyes held a warning. "I can't avoid the council. Eleni was on probation when she came to me—she still is. As my vampiress, the court will have no choice but to be lenient with her, lest they punish us both." His eyes darkened. "I don't anticipate them doing anything so foolish."

He cranked the car then rolled down the window before shutting the door. "If the effects of her turning become... *problematic*, I will take her and leave France. As far as the council is concerned, I have taken Eleni as my bloodmate and that is all they need to know."

"I hope you are right, Julian." Marguerite looked grim. "Really, I do."

He would not argue the matter with her. He rolled up his window and did a loop in the circle drive, making his way out onto the private road. As he pulled away from the house, Julian glanced in his rearview mirror and saw

Marguerite standing in the red glow of the taillights, watching him leave. He had never seen her look so fragile and human.

Forty minutes later, Julian pulled up in front of *l'hotel Pont du Clair*, an exclusive bed and breakfast on the outskirts of Ville Cleménce. Julian knew the owners in passing. Charles and Solange were discreet, reliable hoteliers who had catered to vampire society for over thirty years. He was aware there were least two rooms in the converted farmhouse that could provide a sun-proof rest stop for traveling vampires.

He had called in advance and found out that there was indeed a Liev Sidorov registered there.

Julian parked away from the attached restaurant and climbed out of the car. Inside, the hotel was as he remembered it—clean and simplistic, with romantic amber lighting and faux Persian carpets. Paintings commissioned by local artists decorated the walls.

A young woman with a thin face and piercing blue eyes stood behind the concierge desk when he entered. She called to him, but her voice reached him as if from afar. He had planned to show up at the vampire's room unannounced, but one glance through open glass doors to the dining area on his left, and an onrush of anger surged through him. A vampire with reddish hair sat alone in a booth with his hands around a china cup, idly glancing through a window overlooking the parking lot.

Eleni had described him perfectly, from his smug expression to the prominent, dimpled chin. There was no room for mistake. Julian gestured to the lady concierge that he had found his party then strode into the dining room, his hackles on the rise.

The vampire did a double take as he approached.

"Ah, Sévigné," he said and sat straighter, his eyes dancing with shrewd mirth. "I had a feeling you would come. I heard about the fire at your chateau, an awful tragedy."

"Is it?" Julian made no pretense at civility. He hated the bastard on sight. "One would think you'd be relieved."

He scoffed. "Why would you assume that?"

"Because Gisele Gaspar is dead."

The vampire swallowed convulsively, yet his face remained impassive. It was a long minute before he spoke. "My condolences to her family."

"I am her only family," Julian said in a peevish tone. He leaned forward and glared at the man with thinly veiled hatred. "She was not the only member of my household who has perished."

For a brief second, light gleamed in the vampire's eyes. His brow lifted. "Is that so?" He had the gall to look taken aback. "The fire—your protégé, Eleni—"

"I assure you my bloodmate is very much alive and well. I'm sure that's what Zander Rubio wants to know, is it not?"

Sidorov's cup rattled against the saucer as he put it down, his face ashen.

Julian went on. "Do you think I don't know about your relationship with Gisele? I know you were seeing her before the fire. She had come to the mistaken belief that despite her familial line, she could be made immortal. I never told her any such lies, so I am left to wonder just who put that idea in her head." His brows lifted in silent speculation. "I suppose you would know nothing about that?"

"I'm afraid not. I met your Eleni on one occasion. I have never met Ms. Gaspar."

"That isn't what my sources have explained to me. You were last seen with my servant at a bistro in the square. I have witnesses who can place you talking to her on the night of the festival."

The vampire's lips thinned. Oh, yes, he had Sidorov's attention now. The pale blue eyes had taken on a hard gleam, they darted back and forth as the vampire studied Julian's face.

"Gisele was vulnerable," Julian said, his voice a moody rumble. "She had no ties to you. There is one true connection between my household and yours, and that's between my bloodmate and her ex-Biter—your employer. I would imagine he is also your relative, *hein*?"

"You took in an Acolyte with Biter's Addiction, and you make her immortal? What does that say for your judgment? Such a transformation could awaken a dangerous bloodlust in her. She could attack someone."

"Marguerite was there for her turning."

Tense silence drifted between them.

"You think you are so clever, turning her when she is on probation," Sidorov snapped. "She is still a ward of the council."

"You tell Zander Rubio he is no longer privy to the goings on in my household." He stood up from the table and looked down his nose at Sidorov. "I plan to personally take my bloodmate's case to the council. I am bonded to her, and any judgment laid against her must be leveled against me, also."

Sidorov let out a husky laugh. "Good luck. Her sentence is directly tied in with Zander's."

"I'm sure the council will take that into consideration. I'm sure they'll also be interested to know that Rubio sent one of his trusted men, one of his relatives, to France to gain access to a rival vampire's servant, then manipulated her to the point of misery and murder."

Sidorov's face went slack. His fangs gleamed. "You have no proof."

Julian leaned down on the edge of the table and stared into the vampire's eyes. "I could rip your heart out and send it back to Rubio in a box, and the council wouldn't touch me with the proof I have against you."

Sidorov braced his hands on the tabletop and glared at him in spite. "Eleni Audridov brought most of this on herself, by refusing to settle with Rubio. I wouldn't be here if she weren't so stubborn. The council took away his rights to hold a harem and to take a bloodmate...at least for the duration of Eleni's lifetime. Do you see?"

"I see a motive for murder," Julian grumbled. "And it sounds like Rubio still hasn't accepted his responsibility in Eleni's condition. She didn't bite herself."

The vampire scowled at him. "Regardless of your personal interpretation of the matter, it still stands that the council agreed to adjust their sentencing if a settlement could be reached between the affected parties. Your protégé never appeared at Rubio's sentencing, and after his fate was decided, Dominic Lisandro, your protégé's brother-in-law, lodged a restraining order against Rubio on her behalf. That is why I'm here. Not to try to persuade your house servant. This trouble could have been avoided if your protégé had agreed to negotiate the contract I offered her."

"I would never allow my bloodmate, or any other member of my household, to sign a contract with another Biter, particularly one who is as repulsive and repugnant as your employer." Julian slowly rose to his full height. "I'm of good mind to dismiss you outright and lodge a grievance against both you and Rubio. However, if truly the council has agreed to settle Eleni and Rubio's differences with conditions based on a contract, it's worth consideration just to be rid of the lot of you."

Sidorov took a deep breath and sat back in his chair. "I'm sure the two of you could come to some kind of agreement, regardless of your personal feelings for one another. Say the word, and I'll have Rubio fax another contract to me. I can call him now." He reached into the inner pocket of his dinner jacket and withdrew a cell phone.

"Do you honestly think I would let Rubio call all the shots?" Julian asked him mildly. He reached into his pocket for his keys and began to walk away. At the doorway, he called back over his shoulder. "If he wishes to negotiate a settlement, he will have to meet me in Paris in three days. Regardless if he shows up or not, I'll be taking my bloodmate before the council."

Chapter Twenty

"Where have you been?" Marguerite scolded Julian through the door. She scraped the chain from the lock to let him in and opened the door, greeting him with an accusing look. Tired, he shuffled inside and wiped his shoes on the doormat.

"It's almost dawn. Couldn't you have at least called so I wouldn't worry?"

"There wasn't time," he insisted. "How's Eleni? Any improvement?"

"Not yet."

Julian slithered out of his sport coat and hung it on a peg in the hallway. When he turned, he realized Marguerite stood in a nightgown and bathrobe. She had her crossed her arms over her chest. Was it really that late?

"So, where did you go?" She sounded anything but pleased with him.

"I had business in the village," he said while moving past her toward the kitchen. His body felt drained and his footsteps heavy. He needed to feed and to rest. Then there was the inevitable future he dreaded having to face. "As soon as Eleni awakens, I'm taking her with me to Paris."

"You can't be serious." Marguerite stopped short and gaped at him in disbelief. She followed him through the house. "Julian, she is too weak. We still don't know what her reaction to the transformation will be."

"It can't be helped." He went straight to Marguerite's special refrigerator and tapped a code into the keypad. The digital lock shifted from red to green, allowing him to open the door. He reached in and took out an ice cold bottle of bloodwine. "Eleni's former Biter is probably already on his way to Paris. If not, he will be soon. I intend to be there when he arrives. If I don't settle this now, he will never leave us alone. I don't yet know the entire story, but his representative has been in Ville Cleménce for at least a month—the whole time probably filling Gisele's head full of all kinds of lies. I believe he is directly responsible for Gisele's attack on Claudette and Eleni."

"But what would make her do such a thing...slash poor Claudette's throat like that? The woman was like a mother to her. You think maybe—?" Marguerite hesitated. "Is it possible Eleni's ex-Biter promised Gisele immortality?"

"I wouldn't be surprised. Rubio once promised the same to Eleni, and we're both aware of how that turned out." He crossed to the sink and swiped two glasses from the dishwasher, then carried the lot, wine bottle and glasses to the dining room table.

He sat down heavily in one of the wooden chairs. Marguerite joined him a second later. Elbow propped on the table, she rested her chin in her hand while he cracked open the bloodwine, pouring deeply into the waiting glasses. Julian gulped down half a glass and leaned his head back, closed his eyes.

"I can imagine Rubio might've instructed his representative, cousin, whoever the hell he is, to promise Gisele immortality—whether he promised to convert her himself, or that he'd have a lackey do it, who can guess?" He opened his eyes a fraction, swishing the wine in his glass before lifting his head to take a drink. "Even if immortality had nothing to do with it, I'm certain Sidorov told Gisele that if she killed Eleni, it would benefit her in some way. Money, perhaps. Or maybe, she thought if Eleni was gone, I would take a romantic interest in her." He shook his head. "I don't like to think that's the case, but there it is."

That thought in particular disturbed him, but when he recalled the things Gisele had said to him in the bedroom the night of the fire, it seemed plausible. "It's impossible to know for sure what lies he used to convince her to act," he went on, "but I am nonetheless certain that he is the one who put her up to it."

"Well, do you think the police will do anything? If that man, Sidorov, leaves town—"

"I don't believe he can," Julian said. "Not yet. He's been seen in public with Gisele. Eleni herself spotted them together. The story about the chateau is all over the news. If it's ever discovered that Gisele is Claudette's murderer, and I believe the police will know soon enough, the inspector will have questions for him. He can't afford to run. It will make him look guilty of coercion at the very least. And as a vampire, he definitely can't afford to be caught in the public eye. He wouldn't be able to spend endless hours at the police station."

Marguerite rested a hand against her throat. "There are so many details to consider. Do you truly think he told Gisele to kill Claudette and Eleni?"

"Perhaps not directly, but I think he influenced her in some way, encouraged it, yes." He was quiet a moment, thoughtful. "For years I allowed Gisele to come and go from the house as she pleased. I never once imagined she could do something like this."

"You can't blame yourself, Julian."

"The fact is I could have watched her better. No, no…" He waved her words away when she began to protest. "I could've done more to prevent this. I could've paid more attention to the signs right in front of me." Brow furrowed, he looked down at his hands. "Gita, don't take this the wrong way. I'm not in any way suggesting that you are poorly managing your household. I only want you to be safe. Please take my advice and keep a close eye on your protégés. Not that I doubt the trustworthiness of your darlings, but Rubio and his men are predators. I won't feel good about any of this until after the council meeting."

She reached out and gave his hand a gentle squeeze. "I'll be fine, Julian. So will my ladies. Don't you worry about me."

He would worry, and she damn well knew it. Nevertheless, he let it go. Dawn was fast approaching, and he was tired. He refilled Marguerite's drink, then poured a fresh glass of bloodwine for himself. Weary, he stood up from the table. "I'm going to bed." He eyed the bottle sitting on the table. "You want more of this?"

She waved the bottle away. "*Non*. Take it with you if you like."

Julian offered no argument. Exhaustion was settling in. He took the bottle of wine and slid his hand beneath the bowl of the wineglass, its fragile stem hanging between his fingers, and with no further ado, he started toward the staircase. He'd just passed beneath the archway into the hall when Marguerite called after him.

"Julian?"

He turned to look at her. Marguerite's eyes were filled with worry, and he couldn't help thinking how tired and fragile she looked sitting there in the shadowy corner of the kitchen.

"What are you going to tell Eleni about Paris?"

"You mean why we're going?" He shrugged. "The chateau is gone. I must house her somewhere. If she is not well enough to know the whole truth, that one facet will be enough truth for now. In the meantime, it won't hurt her to know we must live in Paris for a little while. If she needs more time to recover, I will address the council myself, alone. The point is to announce myself as her bloodmate and make arrangements to clear her of her probation. I also want to arrange a settlement of guilt with her former Biter. I want him to have no further reason whatsoever to contact any of us—especially Eleni."

"You must love her very much to do all this for her," Marguerite whispered.

Julian turned to face her fully. "She is my other half. We are connected now. At the very least, I owe her my loyalty."

"But it is more than that," Marguerite said.

"It is." Emotion surged up through him when confronted with the secrets of his heart. "I existed like a dead man until she came into my life. This much you know. But I have lived with a lot of guilt, believing that I am a monster for what has happened in the past. Eleni saw past that. How can I not love her when she has made me whole again?"

His mouth trembled, and he looked at his feet briefly as he struggled for composure. Tears stung his eyes and ached in throat. At least the admission no longer came at the price of his pride. He loved Eleni more than his own life.

Marguerite's eyes were wet with unshed tears. She rose from the table and closed the distance between them and wrapped him in her embrace. "Cousin, you were never a monster."

"I was a monster full of bitterness and hatred," he said against her hair. "Regrets and the past have ruled my life. For far too long"

She backed up, held him at arm's length. "And now?"

"Eleni is my life, my reason for being," he told her fiercely. "I will not let the council ruin her family name to preserve the reputation of a dishonorable vampire. She is a Sévigné now. My name will be her protection."

Nodding, Marguerite let go and daubed at her eyes. "Should I call Eloise and tell her to prepare the townhouse for your arrival?"

"Thank you, *petite chou*, but I've already called her to let her know we would be coming. She sounded happy about it. I think she's been lonely. I've also sent Jean-Pierre notice to have the jet ready tomorrow at sunset. Of course, I will need someone to go with us to the airport. I don't trust leaving my car at the runway."

"I will go with you, of course."

"You have always had the patience of a saint, Gita. I hope you will forgive me for my jealousy of your friendship with Eleni. In my heart, I know you would never betray me." He studied her face. Where would he be without her assistance and wisdom? She was still a little girl in his eyes, even though she was well over three hundred years old. He lowered his head. "I'm sorry I ever doubted you."

"That's all in the past. We won't think about it anymore." She reached up and brushed his hair back from his face, tucking a stray lock of hair behind his ear. "Take heart, cousin. We've made it through the darkest hour. This will all blow over soon. You wait and see."

Eleni awoke with a faint buzzing feeling flowing through her veins, an electric feeling that traveled from head to toe, across her scalp, down her back, and the soles of her feet. Lying in the strange bed, she glanced around the room, marveling at her ability to see in the near perfect darkness. The bedroom door was wide open, and a hint of greenish light fell across the floor near the doorway. Somehow, she was acutely aware it would soon be dawn.

Although she didn't immediately understand how she was different, she felt it inside her. She knew she had changed.

The thirst for blood made her shaky. Her tongue kept touching the razor sharp tips of her fangs. Using what little strength she could muster, she pushed herself up and sat on the edge of the bed and looked at the pale-faced young woman sitting in a corner chair near the open door.

Her eyes were wide and afraid. Eleni couldn't help noticing she had a graceful neck, slender and white. Her hair was pulled back so tightly, the color was indeterminable, possibly a light brown or a dark blonde shade. The hairstyle and the shadows made her pale face stand out—a perfect oval, with glittering dark eyes. To Eleni, she looked like a frightened ballerina.

She was clearly an Acolyte, her face and form could have been a portrait example of exquisite breeding. She also looked frail enough to break.

Eleni felt her mouth water, and without so much as a thought, her fangs elongated. She took a deep breath, and lowered her head. "I want to see Julian."

The Acolyte bolted from the chair and out the door. Her footfalls echoed, and then Eleni heard the cushioning of creaky boards as the woman hurried down a flight of stairs. Then silence. The door quivered on the hinges, shaving down the pie-slice of light.

It dawned on her that this must be her awakening into the immortal world. The shocking realization brought back a memory of Gisele in her dresser mirror, the blunt pain of the sorry cow striking her with something that had been impossibly solid and heavy.

Her heart began to race, the sound loud to her ears. It alarmed her that she was alone. Where was Julian? Was he her Biter? Had he been the one who had turned her?

Voices were coming up the stairs, accompanied by rapid, heavy footfalls. Weak and shaking, she struggled against a hollow feeling rooted in the core of her stomach and tried to stand, but immediately the room tilted beneath her feet. Eleni reached for the bed, only to find it inches out of reach. She stumbled and slumped to the floor right as the door was pushed wide, letting in a wash of florescent light. From the hallway, she heard Marguerite exclaim in French, and then Julian rushed to her side, his familiar scent filling her with relief and elation as he scooped her up into his arms.

"You shouldn't be out of bed," he said in a voice that brought her immediate feelings of safety and comfort.

She cried out his name, clinging to him in mind-numbing relief as he lowered her onto the bed and sat with her, cradling her, attempting to soothe her. Behind him, she sensed Marguerite backing away, taking her protégé with her as she shut the door.

She was horribly thirsty, her throat dry and scratchy. Afraid to let go of him, she clutched at his shirt until at last he pried her hands away, and kissed them, first one, then the other.

"It's all right now. I'm here," he told her, pressing her back onto the mattress when she tried to sit up.

"Where are we?" she rasped.

"Safe. We're at Marguerite's house. This is my room whenever I stay here." He stood up for a moment, and she started, reaching for him. He was only removing his shirt. She heard the rustle of fabric as he dropped it to the floor. "You shouldn't be out of bed."

Her eyes scanned his face. "I hear your thoughts."

"So you do," he agreed. "What am I thinking?"

She licked her dry lips. "You're worried about me. And you're thinking about Paris."

"What about Marguerite?" he asked as he lay beside her in the bed. "What is she thinking?"

She stretched out on her back, feeling much calmer now that he was here beside her. She concentrated on finding Marguerite. A minute passed, then two.

"Can you hear her?" Julian asked.

A frown creased her brow. "I can't hear her thoughts, but I sense her presence. I know she's in her room, preparing to sleep. She's tired, and worried about the future. That's all there is to tell." She looked at him. "It's not normal that I should feel her. You're concerned about it."

"It took both of us to turn you. We believe it is because of your Biter's Addiction. Your body was resistant to the blood exchange. By outward appearances, all is well. But your turning is a secret we'll have to always keep. You need to understand that. " He pulled a pillow closer, tucking it beneath his head. She felt how tired he was. Like his thoughts and body could shut down into sleep at any moment. "Marguerite is worried that your connection to her could put you at risk with the council, and I believe she is right—if anyone were to ever find out." He brushed her hair back from her face. "I'll never let anything happen to you. That is my promise."

"But you're still anticipating a fight with the council. Why?"

He yawned. "Tomorrow, we're going to Paris. I had hoped to put off telling you, but there is no point now that the blood bond has connected us. I plan to go before the council and request that you be removed from probation."

"You can really do that?"

"I can. I also plan to settle with Zander Rubio." His voice took on a tone of grave seriousness. "Whatever comes of the day, he will never touch our lives again."

"Julian…"

"Yes, *mon amour*?"

She hesitated. "What about Gisele?"

"She is dead." He pulled her head down to his chest and stroked her hair. "She can't hurt you anymore." Relieved, she settled against him, her thoughts blending with his in a swirling mix of images and sensations, memories of the not-so-distant past. It was only when his thoughts turned to Claudette that she realized more had happened than she'd been aware of. She dug for the answer and found a pool of blood and smoke, the Saint Vincent of Saragossa shattering, breaking away in colorful shards as flames devoured the house.

"Claudette is dead. And there was a fire?" She pulled back and looked up at Julian, shocked. "The chateau—"

"It seems I won't be able to hide in that prison of a house anymore." His words made her cringe. She started to sit up, but he wouldn't allow it. "But Julian—"

He pressed a finger to her lips to silence her. "The important thing is that we are together. Now, stretch out with me. I feel your hunger and weariness. I know you have questions, and I'll answer all of them in detail later after you've rested."

Wrapping his thoughts through hers, he pulled her to him and encouraged her to feed. She felt his awareness of her awkward shyness, her mild anxiety of biting him the wrong way and possibly hurting him. But, despite her uncertainty, and lack of knowledge of what she was expected to do, he didn't interfere.

When at last her fangs pierced his throat, Julian shuddered with pleasure. His arms snaked around her, and in the cool darkness of the room, he rolled over with her, pulling her on top of him. In his mind, he shared with her the overwhelming paradise of her bite. In return, her love flowed through him like a river, pulsing with every heartbeat they shared.

The knowledge that she cared for him set him free. There could be no guilt in the past, or in turning her without her permission, if only she loved him. His burdens lifted like a bird freed from a cage. They soared away as his hands stroked her back, as she sated herself with his life force. She drank from him until she could take no more.

"I do," she gasped when at last she released him. "I do love you."

She felt her words pour through him like rays of sunshine. Bright and beautiful, they warmed him clear to his soul.

"Do you feel what you do to me?" he asked, urging her to retain their mental connection. But she could barely move her lips. Sleepy, her hunger satisfied, her body was already tingling with sleep. He caressed her face, told her again and again that he loved her. Her breathing deepened, and he encouraged her to close her eyes, to rest.

Reaching down, he pulled the covers over them both and kissed her brow.

"The sun is rising," he whispered against her ear, nuzzling her hair. He explained to her gently that as a fledgling, it would be impossible for her to deny the sunrise. Her body would react instinctively to the need for regenerative sleep.

Her last thought before drifting off to sleep was the awareness that Julian wanted to make love to her, but her body had exhausted itself during her first feeding. It was too soon. It had taken a great deal of strength for her body to accept the transformation, but he promised her silently that he would make it up to her very soon.

Chapter Twenty-One

The hearing took place two days after their arrival in Paris. They gathered on neutral ground, in a presidential apartment overlooking the Place De La Concorde. It was a luxurious setting for such a decision to take place, but Eleni was aware it would have little bearing on the council. Julian had already warned her they would strictly adhere to the laws of Vampire Society when considering her fate and the conditions of any settlement.

Eight members of the Elder Council were present, enough to hold a quorum—two members from Moscow, four from Paris. Dressed for the occasion in a sleeveless black dress, Eleni stood at a bay window while waiting for the meeting to convene. The hushed voices of the men washed over her—she hardly noticed them. She was taken with the view, and with dreams of freedom from her past. Rather than nervous, she felt numb. Or perhaps that was Julian's feelings overlapping her own. She didn't dare study it too closely. Besides, it hardly mattered. They were of the same mind. They both wanted the same thing—for Eleni to be free from the past. From any connection to her former Biter.

Julian had gone ahead of her, found their seats at the table and worked the room. She appreciated his calm effort, and left him to rekindle old acquaintances and to test the mood of the council. Now and again, he shared his findings with her through their telepathic link.

She instinctively knew the moment Rubio arrived. The feeling in the apartment changed. The air thickened. Pretending not to notice, she sipped a glass of bloodwine and eyed his reflection in the window glass. He passed her without a word, his eyes boring holes into her back.

A moment later, Julian rejoined her. He laid a hand on her elbow and whispered gently, "They are gathering in the dining room, *mon amour*. It's time to go."

She nodded and left her glass on the ledge. Turning, she slid her arm into the crook of his and looked up at her bloodmate's face. Her heart flooded with love for him. She was so very grateful she didn't have to go through with this alone.

"Did Rousseau explain the rules to you?" he asked as he guided her into the dining room, which had been rearranged into a boardroom of sorts, with one long, formal table.

"I'm not to speak to Rubio across the table, and he is forbidden to speak to me," she answered in a thin voice. "We will address my probation first, and then we will negotiate the settlement."

"Good girl." He squeezed her hand and kissed it. "Everything should go fine. Be brave and let's get this over with."

They headed toward the dining room, and had just stepped over the threshold when a blond vampire with piercing blue eyes stepped over to them.

"Julian, old man, it's good to see you."

"Francois Pelletier," he greeted the vampire by name and gave his hand a firm shake. "You look good."

"*Merci, merci*…It's been centuries since you've stepped foot before the council. On many occasions, I heard that you had died. I'm glad to see that is not true."

Julian scoffed. "I'm too stubborn for that."

"I would suppose that is so." His eyes flicked over Eleni. "Is this delectable creature your vampiress?"

"Indeed. Allow me to introduce my new bride, Lady Eleni Audridov du Sévigné."

The vampire picked up her hand and bowed slightly. "*Enchanté.*" He kept ahold on her hand and guided her forward. "This way to your seat, Madame."

Julian followed, and when they reached the table, he held out her chair for her. Eleni took a deep breath as she sat down and scooted closer. She was relieved they were on the opposite end of the table, facing Rubio and his representatives.

Zander glared daggers at her while the rest of the table settled into place and Julian took a seat beside her. In a row along the far side of the table, the Elders sat and waited. Eleni turned her attention to them as the vampire in the center, Grigori Vidam, rapped his knuckles on the tabletop and began to speak.

"I wish to make this a brief affair. We have all been called here on short notice, and I'm sure we all have other responsibilities waiting." His cold gaze regarded Eleni without feeling. "We all know one another here, so there is no pretense. Everything spoken this room will go on record, and will be added to the archives. Anything stricken from the record will be recorded and sealed." Eleni felt a trill of anxiety spiral through her as the Elder looked directly at her bloodmate. "We will start this with you, Julian. For the record, state your business."

"I have entered into the blood bond with Acolyte Eleni Audridov. She weathered the turning with no ill effects, and we are now connected to one another, body, blood, and soul."

Vidam jotted a note on his record book, the same enormous leather book Eleni remembered from before. Again, the Elder addressed Julian. "You have not been together long to have made such an important life decision."

"That is true," Julian agreed. "But I stake my family's honor on her loyalty to me."

The Elder vampire looked taken aback. "I don't doubt that. You, yourself are an Elder. Besides, it was your decision to make."

"And I have made it," Julian said. "It is done. Eleni is my bride, and she now shares my name and lineage. That being the case, I'm here to take full authority over her welfare. She is no longer human and has given me no reason to suspect she suffers from any lasting effects of Biter's Addiction. Just yesterday, she submitted herself to the questioning of this council, and as you all have witnessed, she is as normal and functioning as anyone in this room. Since observing her behavior was the purpose of her probation, I feel it's no longer necessary for the council to keep watch over her. That is my duty as her bloodmate. I wish to see her probation discontinued. It is merely an intrusion on our new life together."

"Let it be known that the council grants full rights to Master Vampire, Julian du Sévigné, and holds him fully responsible for the life and welfare of his bride, Eleni Nikola Anastasia Audridov. There is no law to prevent his claim."

Elation soared through her, and her heart began to race. She felt the focused intensity of Julian's mind and tried to still her jangling nerves. It wasn't finished yet, and she was afraid to hope. There was still Rubio to consider. She clutched Julian's hand to keep her own from trembling.

"We will negotiate the grievances between Eleni Audridov-du Sévigné and Zander Maksim Aleksi Rubio." Vidam jotted down more notes, then looked across the table at Julian. "The situation is this—a highborn vampire has not only lost his right to keep a harem, he is forbidden to enter the blood bond for the length of Lady Audridov's lifetime. The decision, of course, was made while she was human, and it was believed she would have a human lifespan. Since Monsieur Rubio is the last surviving male of his bloodline, it would stamp out an old and revered familial name if we were to allow the ruling to stand as is. That is why I am willing to negotiate a settlement between both parties. Ms. Audridov-du Sévigné, what say you? "

Eleni licked her lips. "I'm willing to enter a new settlement with Zander Rubio if the dishonor against my name, and the shame it has brought my bloodline, is forgiven and stricken from the records," Eleni told him with practiced sincerity. "I will forgive Rubio of his abuse of me, and I will be satisfied to release him from the council's previous punishment on my behalf...on one condition."

"You dirty bitch! You vindictive, rotting cunt, you—"

The sudden outburst made her jump. Across the table, Rubio leapt to his feet and all hell broke out. She grabbed Julian's arm while staring in shock at the violent scuffle taking place at Rubio's end of the table. A tangle of bodies sought to restrain him. Chairs flipped and papers scattered. The council watched, deadpan from their seats, as four powerful vampires grabbed hold of Rubio and forced him down again, seating him roughly into a chair. They held him there until he ceased to struggle, and his representative convinced him to be quiet.

It took several minutes to restore the room to order. Eleni's heart was racing. She watched Rubio seething in silence across the table.

He glared at her with malevolent hatred, but Eleni met his gaze without flinching. She felt nothing. No fear. No regret. Any feelings she might have felt for him in the past were dead. Looking at him now was like revealing the horror behind a nightmare. Without the mystery and darkness behind the caricature, she was no longer afraid. When at last Rubio was calm enough to continue, she turned fearless, determined eyes directly at Vidam Grigori.

"Please continue, Ms. Audridov. What is your condition of acceptance?" asked the Elder.

"No one should have to live for centuries alone," she told him levelly, "but hell could freeze over, and still I wouldn't consent for Zander Rubio to have a harem again. Allow him to choose a bloodmate, instead. If he can find someone to love his black heart, then let her have him. But it shouldn't be anyone from Acolyte stock. Give him a vampiress to deal with. Let him enter the blood bond with someone who is his equal and a match to his power. He'll be able to further his bloodline, and it will ensure he won't be able to treat her the way he has treated the Acolytes that were under his care in the past."

"That would satisfy your grievance with him?" Vidam asked for the record.

"I'll accept nothing less."

Vidam added her response into the Book of Acolytes, then looked to his right, down the table at Rubio, who still hadn't taken his hateful eyes off of Eleni. "Monsieur Rubio, would Madame Audridov-Sévigné's offer satisfy your grievance with her? I would advise you to think about it carefully."

"Allow me a moment's council with my brother," Liev Sidorov said from the end of the table. Eleni had not even realized he was there. Beside her, she felt Julian stiffen and she squeezed his hand, bidding him to be silent.

Sidorov and Rubio argued heatedly in Russian for several minutes until Vidam tired of waiting, and demanded an answer. The argument between brothers quickened until Sidorov threw his hands up in impatience and gave Rubio what sounded like a curt warning. Once again, Rubio looked down the table and glared at Eleni. She could see it in his eyes. He wished a painful death on her with every breath she took, but when finally he turned to the Elder, he relented. "My grievance will be satisfied."

"Then it is done," Vidam said. "Unless there is a reason the Elders of the council feel justice hasn't been served this night, I declare a settlement has been reached." No one challenged the decision. "Very well, since all parties are satisfied, the new agreement stands."

Eleni hadn't felt the need to cry until that moment, but when she saw Vidam write his judgment into the archival book, she felt as though she had been set free after a lifetime of captivity. A sob burst forth, then tears of joy. She turned to Julian, who accepted her with open arms. But his face was still stern, still fixed on Rubio scowling at them from the opposite end of the table.

"I would like to add one more thing—as a footnote," Julian said in a voice stern enough to silence the murmurs that had begun to pass up and down the table. Eleni pulled back and looked at him. Every eye on the room watched him, but he was focused, fixed on no one but his bride's enemy.

"Continue," Grigori said gravely.

Julian's voice dropped to a deadly timbre. "I wish it to be known that if any person from Zander Rubio's bloodline—that includes anyone acting at his discretion, or at the discretion of one of his representatives—should ever approach my bloodmate, or any person that falls under the umbrella of our combined familial lines again, I will consider it a breach of this agreement. Make no mistake, I will declare a blood feud if we are approached again." He leveled his gaze on Zander, who watched him with a hooded expression. "Should it come to that, I will not rest until I kill the source of the breach with my bare hands and bury his bones in my vineyard. As Eleni's other half, that is my solemn vow." He turned his head to look at Grigori. "Write that in your record book, and leave it unsealed."

Chapter Twenty-Two

They returned to the Sévigné townhouse after the hearing, which had dispersed in tense silence after Julian's final statement. Rubio's representatives, most of them his relatives, had rushed from the apartment after the dismissal, perhaps anticipating violence.

Eleni knew Julian believed Sidorov—and Rubio, at least, indirectly—was partly responsible for destroying his housekeeper, his family home, and Gisele's fragile existence. But, at the same time, he placed much of the blame on himself as well.

Eleni understood his reasoning, even if she didn't agree with it. Hoping to comfort him, she sent soothing thoughts to connect with him, to embrace him and let him know that she was there for him, no matter what. It was finished. The hearing was over. Justice had been served. They were very lucky.

Eleni was free, her bloodline was safe, and Rubio could never touch her again. Without that ax hanging over her head, she felt as though the weight of the world had been lifted from her shoulders. Still, it was a surreal feeling knowing she no longer had ties to Rubio. The past was just that—the awful past. Now, she could focus on her love for Julian and begin to rebuild her life as his vampiress.

"It doesn't feel real to you yet," Julian observed from behind her. Until he spoke, she hadn't realized he'd come outside.

She turned away from comforting view of quiet, cobbled Rue du Broc to face him. "It almost seems like a dream," she admitted. "I've been a prisoner for so long. First to Rubio, then to my illness, then the council—" A lump formed in her throat. She gazed at him, tears pricking her eyes.

Her fingers were still wrapped around one of the *fleur de lis* on top of the iron guardrails when he started across the terrace to her, his crisp white shirt unbuttoned to the waist. From somewhere in the townhouse, a faint melody drifted out to her. *La Vie En Rose.*

Her heart brimmed with love for him. Whenever she felt his presence or saw his face, she felt safe, like she had found her true home, and it was by his side. Right when she needed him most, when the emotion spilled over into tears on her cheeks, he was there, pulling her into his arms. Soothing her with comforting words, words of devotion and love. Her Julian—her immortal lover. She couldn't help but marvel at him and feel blessed by fate. Despite all her failings, she had her vampire husband who looked at her with love and trust, as though he believed she was worth fighting for.

"Because you are, *mon amour*," he whispered, reading her thoughts. "If you still aren't convinced how much I love you, I suppose I have no choice but to spend the rest of the night proving my devotion to you." Eleni glimpsed his wicked smile a split second before he captured her lips in a tender kiss.

About the Author

Cora Zane lives in an area a northern Louisiana known as "out in the sticks". She has a soft spot for cuddly animals, vampires, tattoos, internet geekery, horror movies, smutty stories, retro junk, old books, and peppermint tea.

The former P.E.A.R.L finalist is probably best known for her Werekind Werewolves series of erotic romance novellas and short stories, but she has also published many standalone works of fiction, as well as two short story collections, A Trick of Light and What She Doesn't Know.

Her flash fiction and short stories have appeared in several supernatural, romance, and erotica anthologies, including Ultimate Angels: Tales of Winged Warriors, Coming Together: Hungry for Love, Weirdly II: Eldritch, Weirdly III, Never Say Never, The Dirtyville Collection, and Morning, Noon, and Night: Erotica For Couples.

You can find out more about Cora, sign up for her newsletter, and view her entire booklist at

www.corazane.com.

www.ingramcontent.com/pod-product-compliance
Lightning Source LLC
Chambersburg PA
CBHW050018180626
46810CB00002B/476